Boomerang Boyfriend

Sweet Snarky Romance Series, Volume 2

Chris Cannon

Published by CC Publishing, 2024.

Edited by Erin Molta
Cover design by Chris Canada
Cover art from Canva
ISBN 978-1-964956-13-8
First Edition September 2017
Second Edition July 2024

Chapter One

DELIA

I flung a glob of black paint at the canvas, pretending it was Aiden's head.

My best friend Zoe entered the old garage turned art studio in back of my house and pointed at my latest artistic endeavor. "What are you doing?"

I repeated the maneuver and enjoyed the wet splatting sound the paint made when it hit the canvas. "I call this piece 'Artistic Anger Management.'"

"Is Aiden still playing the we're just friends game?"

"Yes, and he's acting like we never kissed." That ticked me off the most. Because we had kissed, and it had been awesome, or so I'd thought. But perhaps he didn't agree.

I studied the black and red modern art project that was the expression of my abject frustration over the object of my affection. "I think it needs some orange."

Zoe frowned. "Maybe you should ask him out."

"Nope. We had one official date, and since then, all we've done is hang out with you and Grant. You guys are attached at the lips half the time, which you'd think would inspire Aiden to try and kiss me, but so far, not so much." And I'd initiated the kiss on our first date, so it was his turn to make a move.

"Sorry," Zoe said. "I could ask Grant to help prod him along."

"Don't you dare." I flung a glob of orange paint at the canvas and watched as it smacked dead center, sending out tentacles of color. "It's not like he's the only datable guy on the planet." And not that I'd say it out loud, but I didn't think I should have to work to make a guy like me. Either he wanted to kiss me, or he didn't.

"Fine." Zoe sat on the wooden bench, which was the only piece of furniture in the room. "We really need to get you a couch. This thing is not comfortable."

"If you're going to decorate the place for me, I want a couch and a coffeemaker."

"Sure, I'll get right on that," Zoe said. "On to more important matters. What do you want to do this weekend?"

"I'm still waiting to hear back from Betty's Burgers."

Things had been a little tight around my house since the washing machine and the water heater had both crapped out in the same week. You'd think appliances would have the decency to die a few paychecks apart, but apparently not, which made me feel bad about asking for money. I'd rather work part-time at Betty's Burgers and Pies after school to pay for my artistic habits than watch my mom or dad dig into their anorexic wallets.

My cell rang. I checked the caller ID. Betty's Burgers flashed across the screen. Fingers crossed, I answered the phone.

One short conversation later, I was newly employed. After hanging up, I played it cool, walking over to the sink and rinsing out my paintbrushes. "So do you want to come with me to Betty's to pick up my uniform?"

"You got the job?" Zoe asked. "That's great."

I put the brushes in the drying rack, turned around, and struck a movie star pose. "You are looking at the new Pie Princess."

"Seriously?"

"I even get my own tiara." The job mainly consisted of serving and boxing up pies at the dessert counter. If anyone eating dinner had a birthday, I'd serve them a piece of pie topped off with a candle while singing "Happy Birthday." So much less complicated than being a regular waitress. The only down side was I'd be working with Jack, Zoe's older brother, also known as Jack the Jerk. He pretty much felt like my older brother because I'd known him forever and had the according amount of disdain for him. ⸗

"Don't tell Jack the good news. I want it to be a surprise. Now let's go pick up my tiara."

"I'm parked behind you, so I can drive," Zoe said with a little too much enthusiasm.

What was that about? When I rounded the house to the driveway, a block-shaped blue SUV sat parked behind my truck. "You got a new car?"

Zoe gestured toward the SUV like a floor room salesman. "Allow me to introduce you to Francine. She's a 2012 Sky Blue Metallic Subaru Forester with many years of life left in her. Or so the used-car salesman convinced my mom."

"That's awesome. I bet Jack is ticked off."

"Not really. They gave him the option to trade in his car, but he said my grandmother's old Honda Accord gets better gas mileage, so he wasn't interested. Plus this way, we don't have to share a vehicle anymore which means, according to my grandmother, we should fight less."

I laughed. "Having your own car won't stop Jack from being an overbearing jerk."

"True, but this worked out in my favor, so I don't care. Now let's go pick up your uniform."

I climbed into the Subaru and buckled my seat belt. Since Zoe's grandfather and father had died from injuries sustained in the same car crash, so I wasn't surprised they'd bought her a super-safe automobile.

"When do you start your reign as the Princess of Pie?" Zoe asked.

"Tomorrow night. So I can't go out with you."

"That sort of sucks."

"You've gotta do what you've gotta do." And secretly, I didn't mind. Hanging around Aiden, trying to figure out what was going on in his brain, had become an unhealthy hobby. Who knows? Maybe I'd meet a great guy while I worked at Betty's. Who could resist a girl in a retro waitress uniform wearing a tiara?

...

JACK

I pulled into the employee parking lot at Betty's Burgers and Pies with five minutes to spare. Sometimes working at a burger-and-pie joint sucked, but I liked getting out of the house, and it wasn't a difficult job. I parked my car and jogged over to the back door. The outdoor grills were up and running. The scent of hamburgers and barbecue drifted through the cool fall air, making my mouth water.

"Hey, Jack." Todd waved at me from one of the grills. "Did you hear Betty hired a new Pie Princess?"

"No."

"I don't know her name yet, but she's hot." Todd grinned. "You should ask her out."

Dating someone you worked with had bad idea written all over it, but Todd, who was a few years older than me and had been dating the same girl since sixth grade, seemed to be under the impression he was my wingman. "I'll check her out."

I headed to the front register, where Betty herself was ringing up customers. "What are you doing out here?" I asked, stepping in to take her place.

"Keeping an eye on the new girl." Betty nodded toward the bakery case to my right. "So far, so good. She's a genius with those ribbons, and she can actually sing 'Happy Birthday' on key."

"That's a plus." Jenny, the last girl who'd been in charge of birthday pie, couldn't carry a tune to save her life. Kids had cried when she sang to them. Not the recipe for a happy birthday.

"It's your turn to spy. Let me know if she has any problems."

That made me feel sort of creepy, but I nodded. "Sure." I took care of the next guy in line while I checked out the girl boxing up a pecan pie and decorating it with some sort of fancy ribbon. Watching her wouldn't be a hardship. She made the retro waitress uniform look good. If she looked as good from the front as she did from the back, maybe I would ask her out.

She turned around and handed the box to the customer at the counter, and my world turned sideways. It was Delia. My younger sister's annoying best friend. The girl who was practically a member of my family. When had she become hot? I blinked, hoping maybe I'd seen wrong. Nope. Same blonde hair with hot-pink stripes, which I'd always thought was stupid. Now, wearing the Pie Princess tiara and some sort of glittery lip gloss, she looked wild and kind of sexy. And that was just wrong.

I focused my attention on the cash register, taking money and making change. God forbid I make eye contact with her and she could tell what I'd been thinking.

When the line dwindled down to zero, I straightened out the receipts and opened the box of Bic pens we kept under the counter to add a few more to the mason jar by the cash register. Customers always seemed to walk off with the pens. Maybe Betty should install those pens on chains, like they had at the bank.

"Are you pretending I don't exist?" Delia's voice came from behind me.

Startled, I dropped the pens, which rolled in all directions on the hardwood. I turned to her and pointed at the floor. "Your fault."

She laughed. "Oops."

I squatted down and picked up half a dozen Bics. "So you're the new Pie Princess."

"Yes. I impressed Betty with my ribbon-curling skills, the fact that I don't mind singing 'Happy Birthday' to strangers, and my complete lack of embarrassment about wearing a tiara." She pointed at the ridiculous silver crown on her head.

"Did that always have pink rhinestones?" I didn't remember them from before.

"No." She framed her face like she was posing for a picture. "I bedazzled it to match my hair."

I snorted. "Of course you did."

A farmer in dust-covered overalls came up to the register and smacked his receipt down on the counter. "I don't have all day, son."

Delia retreated back to the dessert case, while I focused on not cursing the man out. This guy was just a jerk who was in a hurry. He didn't know my dad had died a few years ago and that anyone calling me "son" made me want to punch them in the throat.

I picked up the receipt along with the twenty he'd laid on the counter. "How was everything?"

"Fine." He jerked his thumb toward the dessert case, where Delia was cutting a slice of pie for a customer. "New Pie Princess?"

"Yep."

"Can she sing?"

I'd heard Delia belting out songs along with the radio since she was five. While she wouldn't make it to the final round on America's Got Talent, she wasn't bad, so I nodded as I counted out his change.

He stuck a dollar in my tip jar. "Good to know."

The dinner rush started, and I spent the next two hours taking cash and making change. Out of the corner of my eye, I caught glimmers of hot pink rhinestones or maybe that was Delia's hair. Either way, I ignored it. Delia had been a pain in my ass for more than a decade. She'd come home with Zoe during kindergarten and had never gone away. To make matters worse, she was into the best friend of the tool my sister was dating. Tool was the friendliest term I could use when I thought about Grant. He wasn't quite the asshole I originally thought, but I still didn't like him with my sister.

Chapter Two

DELIA

Over the next couple of hours, it was strange to witness Jack being polite to everyone at Betty's. He'd been a thorn in my side since I'd started hanging out with Zoe. Then again, he was paid to be polite at work, so that didn't mean it was a predominant personality trait.

"If I hadn't seen it, I wouldn't believe it," an all-too- familiar male voice said behind me. I turned to find the object of my possibly unwanted affection, Aiden, studying me with a perplexed look on his face. He wore that look around me a lot. Maybe that was part of the problem. I didn't fit into his people shape sorter.

Zoe stood behind Aiden, holding Grant's hand. This had to be her meddling. Aiden had never been to Betty's Burgers before.

"What are you doing here?" I asked, like I hadn't already figured it out.

"Zoe called Grant and asked him if he wanted to grab a burger while I was at his house, so he invited me to come along." He pointed at my tiara. "Why are you wearing a crown?"

I adjusted my freshly bedazzled headgear. "It's a tiara, and it's part of the uniform when you're the Pie Princess."

"And it doesn't bother you to wear it?" He pushed his glasses up on his nose, framing his coffee-colored eyes.

"Are you kidding? It feels like the accessory that's been missing from my wardrobe all my life." I struck a pose. "Admit it. You think I look awesome."

He chuckled and shoved his hands in the front pockets of his jeans. "You always look good, but that tiara is ridiculous." I latched onto the first part of that statement and ignored the second. A waitress came over to me with a piece of paper. "Excuse me, but you're up, Pie Princess. The little girl at table four wants chocolate cream pie for her birthday, with extra whipped cream and chocolate sprinkles."

"Duty calls. I'll come visit you guys if I can." Turning my back on Aiden, I cut a piece of pie, added a mountain of whipped cream and a dash of chocolate sprinkles. Now where were the birthday candles? I checked all three drawers, and of course, they were in the last spot I looked. Hopefully, Betty wasn't timing me. After adding the candle and lighting it, I was ready to make my debut...but wait a minute...I had no idea where I was going, and the waitress who'd told me about the birthday girl was nowhere in sight. Several of the tables had families with little girls. Crap. I sidled over to Jack. "Which one is table four?"

He looked at me like I was an idiot.

"While you're judging me, a little girl is waiting for her pie."

He pointed out the table without commenting, and I approached the little girl and her family. "Is it someone's birthday?" I asked, because I wouldn't put it past Jack to lie to me for his own amusement.

"It's mine." A kindergarten-aged girl wearing a Hello Kitty dress wriggled in her booster seat.

"Do you want me to sing?" All conversation in the dining room stopped. Good thing I didn't mind being center stage.

"Yes, please," the girl said.

I cleared my throat and sang "Happy Birthday," sticking to the basics, not adding any embellishments or many mores at the end. The little munchkin blew out her candle and dug in. Mission accomplished. Now on to my sales pitch. "Would either of you like to order a piece of pie?" Betty had stressed the order part because she wanted the parents to know that the free pie was limited to one piece for the birthday boy or girl.

"We'll split a piece of pecan," the mom said.

"Speak for yourself," said her husband. "I want my own slice. If you can't finish yours, I'll take care of it for you."

The wife laughed. "Fine. Two pieces." She pointed at her husband. "And if you aren't sharing, neither am I."

"I'll have those right out for you."

I headed back to the dessert case. Zoe waved at me from across the room where she sat with Grant and Aiden. I nodded at her and went to cut two more slices of pie.

When there was a lull of customers waiting for dessert and no one in line to check out, I approached Jack. "I know you'll be painfully honest, so how did I do?"

"If you're fishing for compliments, go ask Aiden."

And there was the Jack I knew and didn't care for. "I'm not asking you to stroke my ego. I'm asking what Betty will think."

...

JACK

What could I say? "Your singing didn't make the little girl cry, and you sold the family extra pie. She won't fire you."

Okay. I was being a bit of jerk, but it was self-defense. I didn't need Delia hanging around and becoming chatty with me. I wasn't here to be her BFF or her personal tour guide on how Betty's Burgers worked. She could pick it up as she went along, just like everyone else had.

"Thanks," Delia muttered and went back to her post.

When my shift ended, I headed out to my car, which was finally all mine. My mom and grandma had gotten sick of Zoe and I griping at each other about whose turn it was to use the car, so they'd bought her a butt-ugly powder blue SUV I wouldn't be caught dead in. The silver Accord had a few dings, but it was still way cooler than Francine, which was a stupid name for a car, if you asked me. Everyone thought of this as my grandma's car. Not me. It was the car my grandpa had secretly taught me how to drive when I was fourteen. I was responsible for several of the dings on the fender, which he'd taken the blame for. Driving the car reminded me of him and made me feel like part of him was still around, like maybe he was watching over me.

I made a pit stop at home for a shower and then headed to a bonfire at Trevor's house. After his older brother had OD'd a few years ago, his parents liked to know where he was at all times. Sometimes it sucked, but it also meant they always had good food, the coolest video games, and the latest movies. Tonight it was supposed to be all you could eat pizza and breadsticks. After working with burgers all day, pizza sounded good.

There were a dozen cars lining the side of Trevor's driveway when I pulled up. The good thing about living in the middle of nowhere is you could park your car wherever you wanted. No need to find a skinny spot between two yellow lines. As long as you didn't mess up someone's landscaping or garden, you were golden.

I parked behind the last car and walked up the gravel drive toward the bonfire I could see out back. The scent of wood smoke filled the air. It smelled like fall. I loved this time of year. It always seemed like a fresh beginning. We were a few months into the school year, and Thanksgiving break was just around the corner.

"Jack." Trevor waved at me from his seat on the split-log bench we'd made this past summer.

"Hey, how's it going?" I asked.

"Pretty good." He leaned back on his elbows and then nodded to the right. "See for yourself."

Two girls I didn't recognize were standing close together. One was a tall blonde with blue streaks in her hair, and the other one was short with long black hair. "That's my cousin Sadie and her girlfriend Emma. They're home from college for the weekend, and they came to visit."

Did he mean they were friends or that they were a couple? Sadie laughed and put her arm around Emma's waist, sliding her hand into the back pocket of Emma's jeans. That answered that question.

Trevor leaned forward and spoke in a quiet voice. "Dude. I know she's my cousin, but that's hot."

He wasn't wrong, but I wasn't going to agree with him. "Pervert. Where's the pizza?" Something warm and furry came and leaned against my right leg. I reached down to pet Rocky, a black lab who was going gray around his eyes and muzzle. "Rocky wants to know where the pizza is, too."

"He's the reason the food is in the kitchen. Last time we kept it out here on the picnic table, he helped himself to half of a large bacon pepperoni pizza, and then he threw up in my mom's closet. She was cleaning dog barf out of her shoes for days."

I squatted down and rubbed Rocky's ears. "I bet you were framed, huh, buddy?" He leaned into the ear rub and sighed. "I bet it was the cat, wasn't it?" He sighed again like he was agreeing with me.

"Nice try, but there isn't that much barf in a cat," Trevor said.

"I believe you." I patted Rocky on the head. "Come on. I'll share some pepperoni with you."

"My mom will kick your ass," Trevor called after me.

"What she doesn't see won't hurt me," I called back.

The pizza was on the kitchen table, and it was being guarded by Trevor's dad.

"Hey, Jack." His dad always seemed happy to see me, which was nice.

"Hey, Mr. Thompson."

"We've got pepperoni, vegetarian, or sausage." He pointed at the different boxes.

Rocky walked up, laid his head on the table, and whined.

"No," Trevor's dad said. "Not after the mess you made last weekend."

In the time it took me to load up my plate, a small puddle of drool had formed around Rocky's head. "Can't he have a little bit?" I pointed at the ever-growing puddle of drool. "Because that's sad."

His dad glanced around. "You can give him the crust, if no one sees you, but nothing spicy."

"Come on, Rocky. Let's go back outside." I pulled a lawn chair over by Trevor. Rocky watched me take every bite. I gave him a few pieces of crust, which he swallowed without stopping to chew. "Rocky says you never feed him."

"He's lying," Trevor said. "We fill his bowl three times a day."

"With dog food. That's not the same as pizza." I snuck Rocky a pepperoni that had fallen on the armrest of my lawn chair.

"I saw that, Jack Cain." Trevor's mom came up from behind me.

"It was one pepperoni." I argued my case.

"If he pukes, you're cleaning it up." She didn't sound mad. Once she rounded my chair where I could see her face, I saw that she was smiling. "How's your mom?"

My shoulders tensed. "She's okay."

"I saw her at the grocery store. She seems to be doing better."

I nodded. "She is."

"Good. Tell her I said hello, and she should call me if she wants to go have lunch some time."

"I'll do that." My mom had practically become a shut-in after my dad and grandpa had died. The only thing she had done was go to work and come home. She hadn't really talked to any of us. She hadn't eaten unless we'd reminded her. It had almost been like she'd died, too, but her body still walked around. Sometimes, when I'd tried to talk to her, she'd stared at me like she had no idea who I was. It had been terrifying. I thought we'd lose her, too. Lately, though, she did seem to be more tuned in to what was going on around her. She talked to us about our lives, and she'd started shopping, cooking, and eating again, so she no longer looked skeletal. I doubted she'd want to go to lunch with Trevor's mom, since she and my dad used to hang out with them as a couple, but maybe she'd be interested.

Chapter Three

DELIA

Sunday afternoon, I sat sketching on the couch in the living room while Bob Ross painted happy little trees on the television, courtesy of Netflix. There was something about that guy's voice and his boundless optimism that always made me feel happy and relaxed.

My cell buzzed on the coffee table. Zoe's name popped on the screen. I grabbed it. "Hey, what's up?"

"My mom wants to have a girl's day at the nail salon. She asked if you wanted to come with us." Zoe sounded like she was super excited but trying to play it cool.

We hadn't done anything like that in ages. For her mom to want to go out and be social, even if it was just with us, was a big deal. "Woo-hoo! I'm in."

"Cool. I'll see you later."

I heard the front door open, and my mom came in wearing her Winnie the Pooh scrubs. "Hey, Mom."

"Hey, yourself." She yawned. "How was Betty's?"

"Good. I know what your answer will be since you're probably going to eat and then do a face plant on your bed, but you're invited to girls' day out for a manicure, if you want to come."

"Ask me again when I'm working days. I ate a protein bar in the car on the way home, so I'm going to pass out now."

"Good night."

"Night, sweetie. Hopefully, I'll be on days next week, and we'll do some girly bonding thing then, okay?"

I nodded.

My mom headed upstairs. I heard the white noise machine go on. It sounded like an industrial size fan that could suck the furniture out a window, but it was the only way my mom could sleep when she worked nights.

My mom was a phlebotomist who drove all over creation drawing people's blood. Sort of a transient medical vampire. My dad was a lab tech, which meant they both worked odd shifts. One of my major goals in life was to have a normal daytime job that had nothing to do with blood or any other bodily fluid and allowed me to eat dinner with my family.

Zoe, or I should say Francine, rolled into my driveway a few hours later. Francine was looking ultra-feminine with her headlight eyelashes. I climbed into the backseat. "I love Francine's new look."

"Thanks," Zoe said. "My mom saw them online and ordered them for me."

"Very cool." I smiled at Zoe's grandma, who sat next to me. She reached over and squeezed my hand, knowing I would understand what a big deal this was.

"How was your first night as Pie Princess?" her grandma asked.

"It wasn't bad. The people were mostly nice, but when it was slow, it was boring."

"Most jobs are like that," her grandmother said.

"When Zoe and I open our bakery boutique, we'll never be bored, because we can always talk to each other."

"You two should come work my booth with me at the Christmas Flea Market. Zoe can sell cookies, and you can sell hand-crafted Christmas cards or ornaments."

"That might be fun."

At the salon, I picked out a hot pink glitter polish with silver flecks. "It will match my tiara." I showed Zoe.

"You realize you can't wear the tiara all the time," Zoe teased.

"I could, but I choose not to because I don't want everyone to be jealous."

Zoe held up a bottle of polish that was blue with silver flakes. "I'm going with Silver Sky," Zoe said. "Because it matches Francine's paint."

"I don't know how you can wear those blue and green colors," her grandmother said. "They don't work on me." She picked out fire engine red. "I'll stick with the classics."

"I like this one." Her mom held up a pale pink that shimmered in the light. Funny how that seemed to sum up their personalities... Zoe's grandmother was outrageous, just like her, while her mom was more reserved.

Once our nails were dry, Zoe's grandmother paid for all of us.

"I can pay for mine," I said.

"Nonsense, you're family."

"Thanks." I'd been around Zoe's family for so long they felt like they were mine. They were home way more often than mine, too. I knew I should be grateful my parents had jobs, but I could never depend on them being there for me due to their ever-changing shifts. Sometimes it sucked.

After our manicures, we went to the Thompson's Apple Orchard to pick fresh apples. I was reaching up into a tree to snag a golden delicious when a guy said, "Where's your tiara?"

I knew that voice. "Aiden?" I turned to see that I'd heard correctly. "What are you doing here?" This wasn't a place I expected to run into him. Outdoorsy, he was not.

"My mother's buying apple strudel. I spotted you, so I came over to say hello."

His phone buzzed. He checked it and laughed. "My mom's text says she's wearing nice shoes and she's not going to come looking for me in the wet grass so I should meet her at the car."

"Now I know where you get it from," I teased.

"Please. Compared to my father, my mother is practically a flower child." He reached out and touched the pink stripe of hair by my right cheekbone. "I'd love to introduce you to him just to see what he'd say about your hair. I better go. See you tomorrow."

"See you."

Zoe bounded over. "Time to share."

I repeated the conversation. "Doesn't that make it sound like he thinks I might meet his parents one day? Like we're dating or something?"

"It does." Zoe scrunched up her face like a strange thought occurred to her. "Do you think he thinks you're dating?"

I counted items off on my fingers. "He's happy to see me. He goes out of his way to speak with me. He touches my face. And he mentioned me meeting his parents. What does that add up to?"

Zoe reached up and grabbed an apple, twisted it, and plucked it off the branch. "I think it adds up to you asking him what's going on."

If I have to ask, then it probably isn't what I want it to be.

I flailed in frustration. "Why are males so difficult?"

"I don't know," Zoe said. "You could ask Jack."

"No thanks. It's not like he counts as a real guy."

"I'm pretty sure he'd be offended by that statement," Zoe said.

"You know what I mean. He's a guy, but he's not datable." I laughed. "Then again, at this point, the odds of me dating Jack might be higher than figuring out what's going on with Aiden."

...

JACK

I took one more ride around the edge of the front yard on the lawn mower to pick up the last of the leaves that had fallen off the trees. This was one chore I didn't mind. I loved the smell of the fresh-cut grass, and no one talked to me while I worked or tried to tell me how I should do something. It was kind of cathartic riding the mower back and forth in nice straight lines, watching the machine suck up the leaves, mulch them, and spit them out the back like fall confetti.

When I finished, I drove the John Deer mower into the shed out back and then surveyed the yard. There was something satisfying about seeing the checkerboard pattern I'd cut into the grass. There were only so many things under my control in this life, and the grass was one of them. My mom, grandma, and sister had all taken off for a girl's day, which meant I had the house to myself. That was rare these days, and since I was outnumbered three to one, it was nice not to be surrounded by females for a little while. A familiar ache throbbed in my chest. My dad, grandpa, and I used to play horseshoes or stand around the grill on the back patio on Sundays. I missed that. My mom and grandma made an effort to include me in whatever they did, but it wasn't the same as having other guys to hang around with.

Whatever. I had the house to myself for a bit, so after a quick shower, I was going to eat something and watch football. I'd just turned on the television when I heard a car coming down the drive. A quick check out the window showed it was Zoe's SUV. Damn. I thought they'd be gone longer.

Sinking low on the couch, I put my feet on the coffee table and turned up the game. The door burst open, and the first person inside was Delia.

"Whoa," Delia said. "Do you think you have the television on loud enough?"

Just to annoy her, I clicked the volume up a few notches. "Very mature," Delia yelled.

I grinned and turned the television back down.

"Jack," my grandmother said as she came in carrying a bag of apples, "we're going to bake pies if you want to help."

Why would I want to bake pies? "No thanks."

My mom came over and sat down by me. She took the remote from my hand and hit mute. "Thanks for taking care of the leaves. The yard looks great."

"No problem." Loud laughter echoed from the kitchen. "I think that's my cue to leave."

"You don't have to go. I can quiet the girls down."

"Can you make Delia leave?" I asked.

She frowned. "I don't know why you two are always at odds."

"I have one annoying little sister," I said. "I don't need another one." My cell rang. Trevor's name popped up on the screen. "Hey, what's up?"

"We're going to barbecue and play horseshoes. Want to come over?"

"Sure." Saved by the cell. I stood up and headed for the front door. "I'm going to Trevor's. See you later."

...

Rocky bounded up to me as soon as I stepped out of my car. "Hey there, buddy. What's up?" He leaned against my leg and looked up at me with adoration as I scratched under his chin. "Who's a good boy?"

His tail thumped against the gravel, sending up a spray of dust. Why couldn't people be as easy as dogs?

He trotted beside me as I walked out back. Trevor's dad was just lighting the grill, which meant the food wouldn't be ready for a while. Good. I could hang out here for the afternoon, and hopefully, the house would be Delia-free and quiet by the time I went home.

"So how are things going with the new Pie Princess?" Trevor asked.

I grabbed a can of soda from the cooler, popped the top, and took a drink. "Work was the one place that was mine. No Zoe, no Delia, just my life. It feels like she invaded my territory."

"I've always thought she was cute. Not my type, with the crazy hair and all, but fun to look at."

"I think the hair is a warning about her personality," I said.

"You're still mad about her putting Nair in your shampoo bottle, aren't you?"

"Who wouldn't be? I lost my hair and my eyebrows." I'd never been so mad about anything in my life.

"You're the one who nuked their lemonade stand by telling people you peed in the lemonade." Trevor reminded me like he was some sort of lawyer.

"As a joke. It's not my fault people are stupid and believed it."

Trevor shrugged. "I'm just saying...it's not like Delia and your sister pulled a prank on you for no reason. And it's been what...seven years since that happened? I think you need to let it go."

Chapter Four

DELIA

Monday morning came way too early. I was grateful for the blue-and-green plaid Wilton school uniform because it took much less effort than putting together an outfit on my own.

As I drove to school, I tried to figure out what was going on with Aiden. Maybe I was expecting too much. My mom told me no guy was perfect. The best you could do was find a guy who made you happy 70 percent of the time. When I asked about the other 30 percent, she told me that was the percentage of time you wanted to hit him in the head with a frying pan.

Aiden and I had started hanging out since our best friends were dating. Now he always seemed to be wherever I went. In the plus column, he was always happy to see me. Maybe I should straight up ask him what was going on, but given his shy-boy personality, that type of pressure might make him cut and run.

I pulled into the Wilton School parking lot and parked in the first available space. As I crossed the asphalt, the crisp fall air made me smile. The campus looked like one of those Ivy League colleges you see in movies. The buildings were made of old brick and blocks of granite. There was even a Big Ben-type clock in the middle of a grassy quad.

Zoe waved at me from our normal spot next to the clock.

Of course, Aiden and Grant were there, too.

Aiden took one look at me and said, "Did playing Pie Princess all weekend wear you out?"

What did he mean? I crossed my arms over my chest. "Are you implying I look bad this morning?"

"Not bad." He tilted his head and studied my face. "Just less awake."

Zoe held a cup of coffee out toward me. "This should help."

"Thank you." I sipped the life-giving brew and waited for my brain to fully engage.

"I know what it is," Aiden said. "You normally wear more eye makeup."

"True." I yawned. Trying to draw perfect mega-winged eyeliner hadn't seemed worth it this morning, so I'd gone with something less involved. "Maybe this is my new low- maintenance style."

"I like it. It makes you look less intimidating," Aiden said.

"What the hell does that mean?" I snapped.

"Never mind." He took a step backward. "You're still scary."

The bell rang, and he took off for class. I turned to Zoe and Grant. "I might be a little crabby this morning, but why would he think I'm scary?"

"He likes everything to fit into nice neat mathematical equations," Grant said.

"And you're unpredictable," Zoe said. "I think it attracts him and freaks him out at the same time. But they do say opposites attract, so maybe it's a good thing."

"Well, right now, it's a ticking me off thing."

"Come on," she said. "We better get to class."

At lunch, Aiden pulled a flat wooden box out of his backpack and offered it to me. "I bought this at the school fundraising auction, and I meant to give it to you, but I kept forgetting to bring it."

I opened the box. It was full of more than a hundred Prismacolor pencils, graphite pencils, and paint markers. "You bought this for me?"

He shrugged like it was no big deal. "When it went up for bid, I thought of you."

"Thank you. So how'd your strudel event turn out Sunday?" I asked.

"The apple strudel was good, but the rest of the day wasn't great."

"Why not?"

He took his glasses off and cleaned the lenses with a napkin before putting them back on. "My dad's a lawyer, so he sees everything as black and white. I disagreed with him about something, and he came unglued. Apparently, being his son means I'm supposed to agree with all of his opinions."

"That sucks. What did you argue about?"

Aiden shook his head. "I don't want to talk about it. Tell me about what you can do with those pencils and why there are so many different kinds."

I used to wonder why Adien wanted to know things, but now I knew it was part of his personality. He liked to understand things and analyze them. It was cool in a geeky sort of way.

"Allow me to demonstrate." I grabbed a graphite pencil and a piece of paper and started to sketch him. I could add color later, if I wanted. For now, I drew the angular planes of his face, his short wavy blond hair, and analytical brown eyes behind his glasses. Then I blended in the hair and shaded his cheekbones. "Graphite is cool because it's soft, so the harder you press, the darker the color. Plus you can blend it to soften lines."

"That's amazing." Aiden turned the picture so it faced him. "Is this how you see me?"

Weird question. "Uhm...that's what you look like."

"No, the guy in the drawing looks way more confident than I feel."

"Let me see." Zoe reached for the drawing and held it up so Grant could see, too. She looked at the sketch and then at Aiden. "That's pretty much you."

"I don't think we ever see ourselves how other people see us," I said.

"Why not?" Aiden asked.

"We all have baggage. When I look in the mirror, I see my grandmother's nose, which she hated all her life. I think it's a good fit for my face, but in the back of my head, I've always known she didn't like it and wished she hadn't passed it on to me."

"There's nothing wrong with your nose," Aiden said.

"My grandmother's sister was prettier than she was, or so everyone says. She died before I was born. My grandmother never felt good about herself because she wasn't the 'pretty sister.' If you asked anyone who met her, they'd say she was pretty, but she never felt that way about herself."

"Sounds like your grandmother could use some counseling," Aiden said.

"Probably, but no one from her generation would do something like that. She firmly believes unless you're bleeding you aren't hurt, and if you aren't projectile vomiting, you're not really sick."

"Your grandmother does not sound like a happy person."

I put the graphite pencil back in the box. "She's just a little strict in her beliefs."

"A little strict?" Zoe said. "She used to scare the crap out of me when I was younger. She reminded me of the grandmothers from fairy tales who cooked children for supper."

...

In art class, the teacher had drawn a seating chart on the board, which was odd because we already had a seating chart. And why were there extra chairs at the tables?

"We've had to combine two art classes, so please find your new assigned seat."

That was weird. I checked for my name and saw it was written in a square across the table from Jack's. No way. It had to be a different Jack, not Zoe's brother. I headed for my assigned spot, and nope...I was wrong. "What are you doing in this class?" I asked.

He frowned at me, like he wasn't going to answer, but then he leaned back in his chair and said, "Mrs. Beck had to go on maternity leave early, and Principal Stephens said her replacement can't come in for another two weeks."

"So they're shoving your whole group in here?"

"Class, I know this is a bit crowded, but to avoid changing everyone's schedule, we're going to have to live in close quarters for a while," the teacher said. "Take out your sketch pads. You're going to draw the person across from you."

Great. I was drawing Jack. "The good news is I don't even have to look at you to do this."

"Just make sure you draw me with hair," he muttered.

I bit my lip, trying not to laugh, but it didn't work. He glared at me. "Don't give me that look. You're the one who told everyone you peed in our lemonade."

"No, I didn't."

"Excuse me?" I knew Jack was a jerk, but I didn't think he was a liar.

"I didn't tell everyone. I told two people, as a joke. Apparently, they were stupid and didn't understand sarcasm when they heard it. I guess it spread from there."

I stared at him open-mouthed for a moment. "Then why didn't you tell us that?"

"How was I supposed to know you'd go psycho and put Nair in my shampoo?"

"I spent days drawing on all the cups and making that banner." I bit back the "you idiot" I wanted to end that statement with. "You had to know I'd be mad."

"Normal people don't draw on paper cups. They just pour lemonade in them. As far as I knew, you were out the cost of a dozen lemons and some sugar."

I could see his point, even if he was being obnoxious about it. "So you jokingly told some idiots you peed in the lemonade, which means you were just being an average jerk rather than telling everyone and being the huge jerk I always thought you were."

"That's how you classify me?" he asked. "I'm a jerk either way?"

"Pretty much." I looked down at my sketch pad and started shading in his cleft chin. "But only the huge jerk deserved the Nair, so as much as it pains me to say this, I guess I'm sorry."

"Is that supposed to mean something to me?" he asked.

And now I wanted to stab him with my pencil. "What's done is done. Accept the apology and move on or don't. Your choice." I glanced up and studied his face, taking in his dark eyes and sandy brown hair. Funny, I'd never noticed how pretty his eyes were with the heavy fringe of lashes most girls would kill for. I continued drawing. When I finished, I didn't recognize the handsome guy I'd drawn. I held it up so I could check it side by side against Jack's face. Holy crap.

Jack was really good looking...handsome even. When had that happened?

...

JACK

Delia had a strange look on her face.

"What?" I grabbed the sketch and studied it. Huh... "If I get lost, I want you to draw my picture for the milk cartons. This is good."

"Thank you."

I handed it back to her. "I guess it's my turn to draw you. Just remember, this is my first art class, so don't expect much." Why did I say that? I was decent at drawing, but Delia was talented. There was a huge difference between those two skill levels, and I hated participating in anything where I knew I was at the disadvantage.

Pretending I wasn't nervous, I used soft strokes to outline her eyes and nose. Her eyes were chocolate brown with flecks of hazel. I'd never noticed that before. And her hair...that was a puzzle. I paused, tapping my pencil on the paper.

"Are you drawing me bald as some sort of fantasy revenge?" she asked.

"No." I tapped the pencil again. "I'm trying to figure out how to show your crazy pink streaks."

"I'm going to pretend that when you said crazy, you meant fabulous...and you can shade some areas darker to show there's a color variance without using pink. It won't be nearly as cool, but it's a good technique."

I tried her suggestion. The end results weren't bad. They weren't good, but they weren't bad. I passed it over to Delia.

"Don't take this personally, but if I disappear, I don't want you to be the person who draws my face on the milk cartons."

"Fair enough." I smiled at her, and she smiled back at me, and all of sudden it didn't seem like she was my little sister's best friend...she was just a pretty girl who made my heart beat a little faster. And I realized I was staring. Time to regroup. "So how do you like being the Pie Princess?"

"It's kind of fun," she said.

"I'm surprised you don't wear the tiara all the time," I teased. "Since you're into that sort of thing."

She laughed. "That sort of thing? Do you mean that I fantasize about being royalty or that I like sparkly objects?"

"I'd go with sparkly objects," I said. "Because you're not known for trying to blend in."

"Anyone can blend in," she said. "I prefer to stand out."

"Mission accomplished."

The bell rang, signaling class was over and breaking the weird spell that had fallen over me. What the hell had I been thinking? Had I been flirting with Delia? Had she been flirting with me? No. That was ridiculous. Delia wasn't an available girl. She was my honorary sister. I told myself that as I watched her walk away. Purposely, I stayed back, not wanting to make small talk or do whatever it was we'd been doing. Because Delia was not datable. She wasn't. Maybe if I kept telling myself that, I'd believe it.

For the rest of the day, I had Delia on my brain. Whatever switch that had been flipped in art class, I needed to flip it back. Fast. Before someone noticed me acting weird.

Maybe she wouldn't be working tonight. I should have asked what her schedule was, but that might've made it sound like I'd hoped she was working when the opposite was the truth. I needed a little Delia-free time to get my head on straight.

Later that night as I crossed the parking lot to the back door of Betty's, I waved at Todd, who was basting pork steaks on the grill.

"So how's the new Pie Princess working out?" Todd asked, like he was speaking in code.

"She can sing, and she doesn't drop pie on people, so I think she's doing pretty good."

"Did you ask her out?"

"Dude, she's my little sister's best friend. She practically lives at my house."

"So." Todd grinned. "What's the problem?"

"You can't date someone who lives with you," I said, "because when you break up, it would be awkward." Not that I was considering dating Delia. That would be all sorts of wrong.

"Vicky and I live together," he said. "I don't see the problem."

I didn't have time to explain how faulty his logic was. Instead, I went in and relieved the waitress who'd been ringing people out. There used to be another guy who worked the front counter, but he'd been recruited to make pie dough in the kitchen, and Betty hadn't hired a replacement. Business was always good, but it seemed like Betty wasn't replacing the people she let go or moved around.

There was a line of senior citizens waiting to check out. They finished dinner before most people even came home from work, which seemed strange. My grandma didn't act like that. She ate dinner with us at a normal time. Plus, it seemed to be a universal truth that the seniors weren't good tippers. They had these laminated cards someone gave them ages ago, which allowed them to figure out the tip at 10 percent. Twenty had been the standard for years. There was probably an updated version online. Maybe I'd print them out and pass them out at the cash register, because better tips would make everyone happy.

I found myself checking to see if Delia was behind the dessert counter, but whenever I glanced over, it was one of the waitresses grabbing pie for the customers. I wasn't sure if I was disappointed or relieved.

Chapter Five

DELIA

Aiden waiting by my truck after school made me wonder what he wanted. I played it cool, opening my truck door and tossing in my backpack before leaning against the doorframe. "What's up?"

"I'd rather not go home and deal with my family. Do you want to grab something to eat?"

Okay. I didn't love the way he made it sound like he only wanted to hang out with me, because he didn't want to go home. Maybe that was the shy guy way of hedging his bets. If I said no, he could pretend it didn't matter.

"Sure," I said.

I followed Aiden toward his beige Volvo parked toward the end of the row. "Do you like Mexican food?" he asked.

"Bring on the chips and guacamole." I loved Mexican food.

Eating and talking to Aiden during dinner was comfortable, but something was missing. This didn't feel like a date. After I ate the last tortilla crumb from the bottom of the basket, he drove me back to school and parked next to my truck.

"Thanks for going with me." He stayed on his side of the car, behind the wheel, not leaning toward me one iota, which meant he had no intention of kissing me. At this point, I could come to only one disappointing and confusing conclusion. I'd been friend-zoned.

Okay. I could deal with that. Given a little time, I probably wouldn't want to badger him with questions about why he didn't think I was datable. But for now, I had my pride, so I'd fake it. "See you tomorrow."

I climbed out of his car and up into my truck with a smile on my face. I started the car and waved as I took off like nothing was wrong. I headed for the highway and focused on not crying tears of frustration. This was not a big deal. Not every guy I liked would like me back. And that was okay. Aiden would make a good friend. But why in the hell wasn't he interested in me? Had he met someone else? Some super-smart girl who was into math and boring colors as much as he was? Maybe I'd ask Zoe. Then again, if she knew anything, she would have told me. Only one thing would make me feel better at this point. Pie.

...

JACK

Delia wasn't working tonight, which was good. I needed some time away from her to get my world back in order. She might have apologized to me, but that didn't change the fact that she was unbalanced. Any guy who got involved with her would be asking for trouble. Once, I'd overheard her and Zoe plot to slash Grant's tires. And while I knew they wouldn't actually go through with it, it was still a little disturbing they'd even suggested it. Normal girls didn't plot vandalization. At least, I didn't think they did.

I was cracking open a roll of quarters when someone set a chocolate cream pie on the counter. I checked the price chart and looked up. And there was Delia. My heart tripped a beat.

"What are you doing here?"

"Pie," she said in a voice that sounded like she was about to rip someone a new one. "I needed pie."

I took the twenty she held out to me and then counted out her change, trying to ignore the fact that she looked like she was about to cry. When I made eye contact to hand her the receipt, I caved.

"Are you all right?"

She sniffled. "No, but I'll be okay." And then she headed out the door.

Well, crap. I glanced around for Betty, and since she was nowhere in sight, I pulled out my cell and texted Zoe: Delia's upset. Call her.

There. That took care of any obligation I had toward Delia as a sister or friend or a coworker or whatever. It was a busy night at Betty's. A lot of people picked up carry-out to avoid cooking on Monday nights. Time flew by. At the end of my shift, I grabbed carry-out for myself, and then I was out the door and on my way home.

When I walked into the house, my grandmother sat in the living room crocheting. She nodded at me. I nodded back, appreciating the fact that she didn't try to talk to me as soon as I set foot in the door. Betty's could get loud.

Some nights, I needed a little quiet before I could relax and do my homework or watch television.

Sitting by myself at the kitchen table, basking in the silence, I polished off two hamburgers and then grabbed a slice of the apple pie my grandmother had made from the apples they'd picked. I'd never tell her, but Betty's was better.

"The pie is good, isn't it?" my mom said as she came into the kitchen in her pajamas and cut a sliver for herself.

"It is." I took a large bite and wondered why my mom was smiling at me. "What?" I asked, wondering what was up.

"That was nice, what you did for Delia."

I shrugged, not wanting to make a big deal out of it.

"Maybe her working at Betty's is like a do-over for you two. You can get to know each other as the people you are now rather than the way you were as little kids."

Nope. Not a good idea. I knew all I needed to know about Delia. Getting to know her better could lead to disaster. I shoved the last hunk of pie into my mouth and nodded like I agreed with my mom.

The next day at school, I ignored Delia and Zoe when I saw them in the hall, thereby restoring the balance of the universe. And then it was time for art class, and the world spun off its axis again. Delia looked like she was trying out for a part in a play. Her eyeliner was ridiculous. "What's with the makeup?" I asked, knowing it was the wrong thing to say as soon as the words slipped out of my mouth.

"Just thought I'd try a new look."

"Why?" Why did anyone think they needed to draw sparkly purple lines around their eyes? And not just around her eyes, but out to her temples like some sort of mask. And her lips were the same color purple. It was strange but oddly sexy. I couldn't stop staring at her.

"Why not?" She shrugged. "Sometimes you have to try something before you know if you like it or not."

I wondered if her purple lips might be something I wanted to try. Son of a...this was not a path I needed to go down. Not with Delia.

She ducked her head. "Thanks for texting Zoe last night."

I turned away and grabbed the sketch pad from my backpack. "No big deal." My plan for the rest of class was to avoid eye contact. I'd pay attention to my drawing and ignore the sexy purple sparkles.

...

DELIA

Jack had turned out to be a decent human being, which threw off my worldview by about 180 degrees. Then again, what did I know? I'd thought Aiden liked me and wanted a relationship. Wrong. I'd promised myself I wouldn't dwell on this unhappy discovery, but I would give myself a few days to pout about it. Then I'd move on and find another guy. A guy who wasn't afraid to be seen with a girl who had hot pink hair.

The whole Aiden debacle had taught me one thing. I'd let the next boyfriend candidate, whoever he might be, make the first move. If I'd never kissed Aiden, I never would have been under the impression that he liked me as more than a friend. Maybe he just kissed me back to be polite.

Don't think about it. Don't think about it. Don't think about it.

Focus on drawing. That's what I should do...like Jack was. He was totally into whatever he was working on, so I took a moment to study him. Funny how he looked so different to me now. If I didn't know him, I'd classify him as a hottie, but since I did know him and classified him as almost-family, I couldn't put him in that category. It's not like he'd ever be interested in me. Not that I was interested in him...because even if he was cute and nice and no longer a jerk, he was still off-limits. End of story.

Zoe's family was there for me more than my own. Not that it was my parents' faults. Food and shelter weren't free, but I wished one of them would get a job with regular hours. Right now, if I had an emergency, my first phone call would be to Zoe's grandma, because I knew she was home during the day and would drop whatever she was doing to help me. So no matter how attractive I thought Jack was, I could never act on it. Because when we broke up, not if, but when—because couples in high school always break up—I'd lose my best friend and my family. And that wasn't a risk I was willing to take.

Time to think of something else. I decided to sketch some clothes. Right now I wished I had some sort of emotional armor to protect me from the disappointment I felt over Aiden friend-zoning me and the strange discovery that if Jack wasn't Zoe's brother, I might flirt with him. As I sat there wondering when my life had turned into fodder for a sitcom, I drew a quilted leather bomber jacket fashioned after a knight's armor. Not that I knew how to work with leather, but some day I would. Given enough cash to buy supplies and a few instructional YouTube videos, I could create anything.

When the bell rang dismissing class, Jack almost ran from the room. Was he going to meet someone? I hadn't seen him with a girlfriend, but that didn't mean anything. He probably wouldn't hang out with a girl at school or hold her hand in the hallway. He didn't seem like the sentimental type.

Zoe waited for me by my car after school. "Want to go get coffee somewhere?"

"Let's go to The Art of Tea." The tea shop turned artist's studio was one of my favorite places. People donated leftover art supplies, and anyone could paint or draw whatever they wanted. Maybe there'd be a cool group project I could work on.

"I'll meet you there," she said.

Fifteen minutes later, raspberry tea in hand, Zoe and I sat at a table by the bay window.

"What are you going to paint?" Zoe asked.

I checked the wall of partially finished paintings and noticed one with blue and green waves. It looked like someone was trying to draw the ocean but had forgotten the beach. "I see what I want." Before I could walk across the room and grab the painting, a man with a white goatee snatched it off the wall.

An old Rolling Stones's song that my mom liked played tauntingly in my brain. "You Can't Always Get What You Want." My subconscious was hilarious. Fine. "Maybe I should start something new."

Zoe sipped her tea while I sorted through the different blank canvases or canvases someone had painted over. A canvas which had been painted all black caught my attention.

When I returned to the table, Zoe was crocheting one of her awkward scarves. She never looked at patterns or counted her stitches, so the end product was always a bit misshapen. She didn't care, and the scarves still kept your neck warm, so it worked for her.

I placed the black canvas on the easel and dipped my brush in gray. Without a plan, I started painting lines that curved and turned back on themselves, going nowhere.

"Is that a metaphor for how you feel about Aiden?" Zoe asked.

The back and forth twisting lines did remind me of all the speculating I'd done over whether Aiden liked me, the highs and lows of our not quite a relationship status. It could also represent my strange new realizations about Jack, but Zoe didn't need to know about that. "I guess so."

"I asked Grant who Aiden dated in the past, and he said Aiden normally hangs out with girls for a while, but he's never really referred to any of them as his girlfriend."

"Aiden's a player? Seriously?"

"No. Not like that." Zoe stopped crocheting to pick a snarl out of her yarn. "Maybe he's just terminally shy or maybe since he's male and therefore not fully emotionally evolved, and he doesn't understand how relationships are supposed to work."

By their senior year, most guys have had at least one girlfriend. "Maybe his shy geek-guy personality is just a ruse to get girls to come on to him," I said. "That way he doesn't have to do any of the work."

"I doubt that. The boy is seriously awkward. When I made him come to Betty's with us, he muttered under his breath the whole drive over. It sounded like he was practicing what he might say to you."

"He didn't have much to say to me today." At lunch, we normally chatted about stuff. Today he'd been quiet, too quiet, like he was thinking about something.

"Grant said Aiden was kind of out of it today. I think he had a fight with his dad last night."

I set my paintbrush down and sipped my tea. "My first instinct is to call and see if he's okay, but that's not really my job, is it?"

"As a friend, it could be your job," Zoe said.

"I'm not sure I'm ready to play that part yet. I'll get there eventually, but first I need to get over this angry, rejected, why the hell doesn't he want to kiss me feeling."

"And I know how to help you get over that feeling. We just need to find a single guy who you think is cute."

I'd already found one. One that could never work. Anyway, I didn't need a guy in my life. "Honestly, I don't want to go searching for a guy. If I meet someone, that's fine, but right now I'm going to concentrate on me. I need to work on something I can sell at the Christmas Flea Market. Your grandma offering to share her table is a big deal. You have to reserve those things more than a year in advance. I don't want to let her down."

"I can't bake my cookies until the day before, so I can help you with whatever you want."

"Let's brainstorm." I sat down at the table and hugged the mug of tea to my chest, inhaling the raspberry-scented steam. "I could make cards or paper ornaments."

"You could make cool gift bags. Just buy the solid- colored bags and draw on them."

"People throw those away. I hate to think of spending hours on something that would end up in the trash the day after Christmas."

"People throw cards away, too," Zoe pointed out.

"Then I guess I'm making some kind of ornament."

"We could buy solid-colored glass or plastic ornaments, and you could paint on those."

"I like it. And just to keep from worrying about breaking them, I say we go with the shatterproof kind. I could draw on them with paint pens." Having something to focus on made me feel better.

...

JACK

Friday after school, all I wanted to do was to take a nap and then go hang out at Trevor's. I was about to doze off in my room when loud laughter drifted up from the kitchen below. I liked my room because it was bigger than Zoe's, but being over the kitchen wasn't always great. The sound came right through the heating vents. I'd never told anyone I could hear most of what people said if they were sitting at the kitchen table, because sometimes it came in handy. Right now, it meant I could hear Delia and Zoe talking about some stupid Christmas ornaments they were painting.

I put my pillow over my head, trying to muffle the sound. It worked, but the feeling that I might suffocate didn't promote restful sleep. I flung the pillow to the floor and sat up. Why couldn't Zoe go hang out at Delia's house? Was that too much to ask?

Giving up on a nap, I headed downstairs.

"Someone looks crabby," Delia commented as I walked into the kitchen.

"Someone was trying to take a nap until you guys started talking non-stop." I poured myself a glass of milk and turned my back to them as I drank it.

"You should get some noise-canceling headphones," Delia said.

"Or you guys could hang out at your house." I put my empty glass in the sink. "I swear sometimes it's like you live here. And now you're at Betty's, and we're stuck together in art. In case you didn't realize it, a little of your personality goes a long way."

Delia sucked in a breath and looked at me with impossibly large brown eyes, and then she looked down at the ornament she was painting.

Damn it. "This is the part where you're supposed to yell back at me and tell me I'm a jerk," I reminded her.

Delia didn't look up. She just drew swirling lines on the ornament. I might have heard her sniffle.

"What's wrong with you?" I asked.

She glanced up at me. "That is a very good question. Right now my only response is, 'Go to hell.' I'll get back to you about the rest of the answer when I figure it out."

"See," I said. "That's how you're supposed to act." Walking out of the kitchen, I felt better about our relationship. I'd insulted her; she'd told me off. The balance of the universe had been restored.

On the drive to Trevor's house, the image of Delia with those big brown eyes, looking like she was about to cry, chipped away at my good state of mind. I wasn't the reason she was upset. Someone else had ticked her off, and I'd been caught in the fallout. I had nothing to feel bad about. It probably had something to do with that Aiden guy she liked. It was Friday night. The guy probably hadn't asked her out and she was ticked off. Before the night was over, she'd probably be making plans to blow up his car.

Trevor sat in a lawn chair by the bonfire out back. He had four hot dogs in a roaster he was holding over the fire. Fat dripped off the meat and sizzled in the flames, making my stomach growl.

"I call dibs on two of those." I sat in a chair next to him. "Sorry," Trevor said. "Two are for me. Rocky has dibs on one, and you can have the one that's left."

Rocky had his head on the arm of Trevor's chair with his eyes locked on the hot dogs.

"I see what you mean." I reached over and patted Rocky's head. "I won't try to steal your dinner."

"Good thing," Trevor said. "This is one vicious attack dog. He'll take your arm off."

I leaned back in my seat. "Only if you're trying to pull food from his mouth."

When the hot dogs were done, I ate one and then put four more on the roaster. Trevor cut Rocky's hot dog in pieces and put it on a paper plate in the grass.

I watched as Rocky gobbled up the meat and then started chewing the plate. "The plate's not food," I told him.

"Rocky, give it." Trevor held out his hand.

The dog hung his head and looked at Trevor with big sad eyes.

"You're not in trouble, dude, but you can't eat the plate." Trevor pulled the plate from his mouth or what was left of it.

"Make sure you shut the door to your bedroom before you go to sleep tonight," I said.

"Nah. He sleeps with me." Trevor patted Rocky. "And we have a deal. He can throw up anywhere but my room. Right, boy?"

Rocky barked.

"If I got a dog, do you think he'd be as good as Rocky?"

"Nope. He's one of a kind." Trevor scratched the dog's ears. "But you should get a dog. You're dog people. Rocky says so."

"Maybe now that my mom's feeling better, I could get a dog." Having someone who'd be happy to see me every time I came home would be nice.

Chapter Six

DELIA

"Good thing we bought the shatterproof ornaments," I said.

"Why?" Zoe asked.

"When I throw them at your brother, they won't break. And they're probably more aerodynamic, so I'll be able to aim better."

Zoe finished painting ivy on a silver bell. "If Jack wasn't a jerk, we wouldn't recognize him."

"But that's just it," I said. "At work he's polite to everyone, and in art class he isn't bad. It's just here at home that he's an aggressive jackass."

Zoe set her ornament down. "It's funny you should say that. At school he does seem like a decent guy, but at home he's a tool."

"So what's here that makes him so crabby?" I asked. "I mean the answer could be me, but I'm around him at two other places where he's okay."

"What do you two look so serious about?" Zoe's grandmother came into the kitchen and poured herself a glass of white wine.

"Jack," Zoe said. "He's decent at school and at work, but he's so crabby at home. Why do you think that is?"

She sipped her wine and leaned against the counter. "I don't know. Maybe because he's the only male. I think that's hard on him sometimes."

Well, crap.

"I never thought about it like that," Zoe said. "And I kind of feel like a jerk for not thinking about it. I still have you and Mom, but he doesn't have Dad or Grandpa."

"He does spend a lot of time over at Trevor's," her grandmother said. "Not that it would make up for the loss, but it has to help a little bit."

"Maybe Jack's right," I said. "We should hang out at my house more often to give him some space."

"Do you think that would help?" Zoe asked her grandmother.

"I don't know. You could try it and see." Her grandmother headed back into the living room.

"Why don't we hang out more at my house?" I never really thought about it. When we were younger with my parents working odd shifts, I had stayed at Zoe's out of necessity. My mom had offered to pay Zoe's grandma for taking care of me, but her grandmother had refused. Now that we were older, it didn't really matter whether my parents were home or not.

Zoe held the ornament she'd been working on up to the light, inspecting her work. "Maybe we don't hang out there because we always end up baking something, and by we, I mean me, and I know what ingredients are here."

"Because your grandmother stocks the house with enough food to withstand the zombie apocalypse and my mom only grocery shops at random intervals and buys whatever she's in the mood for?" The only staples you could count on being stocked at my house were Pop-Tarts and protein bars because my parents needed portable food. "The answer is simple. When you pack your clothes, you can pack the ingredients for whatever you want to bake."

Zoe gave me the side-eye. "Do you remember the last time someone used the oven at your house?"

"Now that you mention it, I think my mom's using it as storage for the pots and pans, but the Crock-Pot gets regular workouts. Can you bake cookies in that?"

"No...but I've seen recipes for lava cakes in Crock-Pots."

"And we have a plan. Next time we spend the night, you'll stay over at my house and we'll make lava cake."

Zoe set her ornament down on the table. "Speaking of cake." She stood and went to the counter and plugged in the Kitchen-Aid mixer. "What sounds good?"

I continued painting as she dug out ingredients. "You know my rule. Any flavor of cake works as long as the icing is chocolate."

"I'm thinking chocolate butter cream frosting on vanilla cake."

"Yum." My phone rang. Aiden's name flashed on the screen. What did he want? Only one way to find out. "Hello?"

"This is going to sound weird, but I need to talk to someone, and you're the first person I thought of."

My heart beat faster. "Is something wrong?"

"Yes and no. Grant said you and Zoe were hanging out at her place. Can I come over?"

"Hold on." I told Zoe about Aiden's weird request.

"Couldn't hurt to see what he wants," Zoe said.

So I gave Aiden directions to Zoe's house and then compulsively checked the time on my phone every ten minutes. Forty minutes later, I slumped in my seat. "Shouldn't he have been here by now?"

"Depends on where he was when he called. Did he say?"

"No."

My cell buzzed, startling me. I picked it up and frowned at Aiden's name. Had he decided he didn't need to speak to me? "Are you lost?"

"I was lost." Aiden's irritation came through the phone. "Now I'm at Betty's."

"Why are you at Betty's?"

"Because apparently Google recognizes it as a sign of civilization, but it doesn't recognize the road that leads to Zoe's house."

I almost laughed but managed to suppress it. "You sound stressed."

"I am, and talking to you isn't going to change anything, so I think I'm just going to head home."

He was upset, I understood that, but he was kind of being a jerk. "What's your problem?"

"I wanted to talk to you, but I don't want to do this over the phone. Another time, okay?"

Before I could respond, the dial tone came through loud and clear. Okay then. "I think it's time for me to focus on finding another guy."

"There are plenty of fish in the sea," Zoe said. "You might meet Prince Charming at work."

"Right, like some guy is going to see me dressed as the Pie Princess and fall madly in love with me." A picture of Jack with a crown on his head appeared in my mind. What in the heck was that about?

...

JACK

I griped a lot about working Saturday nights, but it kind of made my life easier. I didn't have to worry about asking a girl out on a date and being rejected. Not that I struck out a lot, but sometimes it didn't seem worth the trouble.

And I hadn't met a girl lately who seemed worth the trouble. One problem with small towns was that after a while, you knew everything about everyone and it limited your dating options.

Melissa Hicks flirted with me at school, and she was cute, but to me she'd always be the girl who threw up on the Popsicle stick log cabin I brought for show and tell in kindergarten. It's not like I held that against her, but it didn't land her in the most desirable female category.

Speaking of non-dateable females, Delia was behind the dessert counter when I came in. I gave her the obligatory head nod that was required to be polite, but I planned to avoid her. The steady stream of Saturday night customers kept me busy enough that it wasn't a problem.

And then I took a break, which meant I grabbed a burger and a sweet tea and headed to one of the picnic tables out back. It was cool enough that not a lot of people chose to sit outside, which was fine by me, but there were a few other people with the same idea, and one of them was wearing a tiara. Maybe I should go back inside.

Todd sat across from Delia. He caught sight of me and waved. So much for making a quick exit. I came over and sat next to him and took a giant bite of my burger so I wouldn't have to make conversation.

"Delia was telling me she's friends with your sister," Todd said.

I'd already told him that. He was either making small talk or trying to mess with me. I wasn't sure, so I nodded and continued chewing.

"Do you know any deep dark secrets about Jack I can use against him?" Todd asked.

"Not really," Delia said. "We mostly avoid each other. He thinks I'm annoying."

The other occupants at the table looked at me like I was a jackass. I swallowed what I was chewing and wiped my face with a napkin. "Way to throw me under the bus."

"Am I lying?" she asked.

I thought about what my mom had said the other day. "The Delia that used to steal my GI Joe doll for Barbie weddings was annoying as hell. Now, you're not so bad."

"Gee, thanks." She finished off her soda. "I guess you aren't as obnoxious as you used to be, either."

Rather than commenting, I ate my burger and fries. Delia checked her cell and frowned.

"What's wrong?" Todd asked.

"Nothing." Delia cleaned up her mess and headed back inside.

Todd elbowed me. "Go talk to her. Find out what's wrong."

Right. "If she wanted to talk about it, she would have." And it was probably something to do with that Aiden guy, which meant it was something she'd talk to Zoe about, not me. Not my job.

Todd stood. "My break is over. Back to the grills."

Betty kept the outside grills going until the snowstorms hit. I inhaled the cool smoke-scented air. We probably only had a few more weeks before winter really kicked in.

My cell vibrated with a text. I checked. It was from Trevor. He sent me a picture of Rocky. At least I assumed it was Rocky. It was a little hard to tell since he was wearing a Cheerios box on his head.

I texted back: Looks like he's happy.

A picture of Rocky with cheerios stuck on his nose and mouth came next. He didn't appear upset.

He's always happy, Trevor texted. Until he throws up. Come over after work. You can be on dog-barf watch with me.

I laughed and texted back: See you then. If he throws up, you're on your own.

Fine, he texted. Meet me at Edison's instead.

The rest of the night went by pretty fast. When I had half an hour left on my shift, Aiden came in by himself and stopped at the dessert case. Delia didn't look excited to see him. They must not be hitting it off.

I tried to eavesdrop, but the noise level of Saturday night kept me from hearing what they were saying.

Chapter Seven

DELIA

Saturday nights were loud and busy. Not that I minded. Keeping busy kept my mind off a certain confusing someone, or rather two confusing someones. I was beginning to realize that for whatever reason, Aiden and I were no longer on a path toward romance. And he'd become obnoxiously needy lately. And Jack...when he'd said I didn't annoy him anymore and smiled at me, my heart had skipped a beat, which was wrong. My heart and my hormones needed to cool it. Jack was not datable. He wasn't. Which left me with jack-squat for love interests. Good thing I worked in a place where I could drown my frustrations in pie. I finished decorating a pie box with ribbons and then turned around to find Aiden at the dessert counter.

Startled, I dropped my scissors. After retrieving them, I said, "Can I help you?"

He shoved his hands in the front pocket of his jeans and then looked down at the floor as he spoke. "I was hoping you'd want to go grab a coffee or get something to eat after work." He glanced up at me. A mixture of hope and guilt shone from his eyes.

"Not coming to see me after you called me was a crappy thing to do." And he needed to know he couldn't treat me like that, even if we were just friends.

"I know, and I'm sorry." He moved closer to the counter. "Not being able to find Zoe's house when I'd been there before was more than my male pride could take."

"And since you're a guy, you have that pesky no stopping and asking for directions gene."

"True." His face relaxed into an easy grin. "To show you how sorry I am, I'm even willing to go to that tea place with the looms."

That was saying something. "Maybe we'll save The Art of Tea for when you really make me mad." I checked the pie shaped clock on the wall. "I'm off work in twenty minutes. We'll figure out what we're doing then."

43

"Cool." His posture relaxed. "I'll wait over there."

Aiden wandered over to the benches in the entryway where people waited when there weren't any open tables. He pulled out his cell and started tapping on the screen. I glanced over at Jack. He was smiling and talking to customers as they checked out. Was it weird that I now thought Jack was better looking than Aiden? Not that I planned to move on to Jack, because that could never work...

It might be best to deal with one problem at a time. At the moment, I had a decision to make. Should I ride with Aiden or follow him in my car? If I rode with him and what he said upset me, I'd have to endure a not fun car ride back to Betty's to pick up my truck.

Maybe I should suggest someplace close just in case. Exactly twenty minutes later, Aiden walked back up to the dessert counter and said, "Why do you look like you're plotting something?"

"Because I am."

"Okay. What are you plotting? How to make tiaras a fashion trend?"

"Tiaras...world domination...the usual."

"Just your normal Saturday night?"

"Exactly." I came out from behind the counter. "I suppose I can put off taking over the world for a little while, if you want to go have pizza. There's a place about ten minutes from here."

"Is it on a road Google Maps recognizes?" he asked.

"Probably. Just to be safe, I can drive my truck, and you can follow me."

"I'll drive. You can navigate."

Once we were in his car, I had a change of heart. "Forget the food. I need to know what's going on."

He sighed. "Okay. Listen...I like you a lot, more than I've liked other girls."

"Then what's the problem?" I didn't get it.

He reached over and held my hand. "I can trust you, right?"

"Yes."

He leaned in closer. "I mean it. If I tell you what's going on, you can't tell anyone, not even Zoe."

I yanked my hand from his. "Then maybe you shouldn't tell me."

Disappointment shone from his eyes. "Seriously? I'm about to share a secret I've never told anyone, and you don't want to know unless you can tell Zoe?"

Now I felt like crap, which wasn't fair. "I've never kept a secret from Zoe. She's my best friend."

"I don't rank as high as Zoe, I understand that, but... never mind...this was a stupid idea."

Oh really? "You don't get to be mad at me. You're the one who kissed me and then friend-zoned me."

Aiden gripped the steering wheel so tight his knuckles turned white."If you could keep from telling Zoe, I'd explain why."

Could I not tell Zoe something? "What's so terrible that she can't know?"

"It's not terrible. It's just that I don't think Grant will understand. I'm not ready to tell him yet."

Aiden looked miserable. Part of me was glad. The other part of me knew I should be a better person. "Fine. I won't tell Zoe."

"Thank you." He released the steering wheel. "It's not that I don't want to date you. You're great. It's that I don't think I want to date girls."

What did he mean...and then I understood. "Okay." That's all I could manage for the moment. My brain sputtered. Aiden was gay? That's why he didn't want to date me? If that were true, then why had he gone on a date with me and kissed me? Why not tell me up front?

"That's all you have to say?" he asked.

"Okay?"

"Give me a minute." What could I say? This gave the situation a whole new spin...still not in my favor, but at least I wasn't the reason he didn't want to date anymore. At least I didn't think I was. It's not like kissing me made him decide dating guys was a better option. Right? "So...was I some sort of test case to see if you liked girls?"

"No. I like you. You're a mystery. You make me think. If I could like any girl, I think it would be you."

"That is oddly flattering and offensive at the same time."

"Please tell me we can still be friends," Aiden said.

I nodded. "Yes. We can. And the it's not you it's me excuse really does apply in this case."

"Thank you for understanding," Aiden said. "I have no idea how to deal with this."

"So you just sort of figured this out?" I asked.

"I've kind of suspected for a long time." He shrugged. "But with my dad...let's say it's not something I can share with my family."

"Your secret is safe with me." There was something I needed to know. "If I hadn't kissed you at Edison's, would you have kissed me?"

"Maybe, but you taking the lead made things easier."

"So when I kissed you, there was no spark?" Because I thought it had been awesome. What did that say about me?

He grinned. "There was some, but not as much as there should have been."

How could he gauge that? "So...have you kissed a guy? I mean, how do you know that's what you want?"

"I went to computer camp this past summer," Aiden said, "and there was this guy, Lawrence."

"And where is Lawrence now?"

"In California, where it's a lot easier to date whoever you want," Aiden said. "I want to go to college somewhere like that, where you don't have to hide who you are."

Canton, Illinois, wasn't the most progressive place, but it wasn't completely backward. "You know the guys who own Canton's Crafts are a couple, right? And I've seen some guys holding hands at school in between classes."

"Their fathers must not be as narrow-minded as mine." Aiden adjusted his glasses. "I think my mom knows, and she's okay with it. When we bought strudel the other day, she asked me if I thought the guy behind the counter was cute."

"Maybe that's her way of telling you she's okay with you liking whoever you want."

"My dad's not. He likes to complain about the new marriage laws."

"Wow. That must be awkward."

"You have no idea." Aiden reached over and grabbed my hand. "Thanks for not hating me."

I squeezed his hand and then let go. "I could never hate you, but this still kind of sucks. And Zoe is going to ask why we aren't dating. What do I tell her?"

"Tell her we decided we're better off as friends. That way we can still hang out with them until one of us starts dating someone else, and by one of us I mean you, because until I move out of my house, away from my father, I'm going to have to hide what I want."

I felt bad for him, but I felt bad for me, too. Who would I date? I couldn't remember the last guy I liked as much as Aiden. Maybe I hadn't been looking because I'd been focusing on him. Maybe if I opened my eyes and took a good look around, the perfect guy might be closer than I realized.

"Do you mind if we don't go grab something to eat?" he asked. "I've been worried about this for so long, now all I want to do is go home and relax."

"No problem." I kind of needed some time to recover from this bombshell, too.

"Cool. See you tomorrow."

I exited his vehicle and headed over to my truck. Now what? I didn't want to go home to an empty house. While I wasn't mad at Aiden, I was a little ticked off at the universe. Why did I have to cross paths with such a great guy who'd never be interested in me? It almost felt like I was the object of some cosmic joke. What could I do to burn off this layer of frustration and clear my head? For now, maybe I'd just drive and figure it out as I went along. Funny how that sounded like the plan for my life. Me, by myself, stumbling along trying to figure out which way to go.

...

JACK

Why was I sitting in my truck, spying on Delia and Aiden? I hadn't planned it, but the timing just worked out that way. Through the windshield, I could see them talking. Delia wasn't crying, so she couldn't be too upset. I should just pull out and drive home. It's not like I didn't have anything better to do. I was meeting Trevor at Edison's in half an hour.

Delia climbed out of Aiden's car, jogged over to her truck, and climbed in. I waited for her to start the engine and pull out of the lot before I headed out myself.

I ended up being a few minutes late to meet Trevor. He was already riding a motorcycle attached to a machine. I slid my card through the scanner and climbed onto the motorcycle game next to his.

"You're late," he said. "Was there a burger emergency?"

I turned the handle, revving the engine. "That joke was old a year ago."

"If it's funny once, it's funny forever," he said.

"No. It's not." I wasn't one of those guys that quoted movie lines all the time, and I didn't like idiots who did. Just because someone wrote a funny line didn't mean it was funny if someone randomly repeated it. Not that Trevor agreed with me.

He leaned into a turn, and his bike tilted sideways. "If there wasn't a burger emergency, did anything interesting happen?"

I gunned the engine and took off. "I think Aiden friend-zoned Delia."

"Does that mean you're interested?" Trevor asked.

"No." I leaned left as I raced around the track. "It means nothing more interesting than that happened. People ate food, paid me, and I gave them change."

"As my dad likes to say, 'If it's fun, they wouldn't have to pay you to do it.' Speaking of jobs, are you going to the career fair after Thanksgiving?"

Just because it was my senior year didn't mean I had a clear cut plan about what I wanted to do with my life. "I think I want to check out the engineering programs."

"You did always like to build with Legos," Trevor said.

I laughed. "I was a master builder. I wonder what degree you have to get to work for Lego."

"That would be a cool job," Trevor said. "My dad thinks I should check out what programs are offered at the triple C. Maybe they have a Lego major."

Everyone called Canton Community College the triple C because it was easier to say. "You know they want you to go there so you'll stay at home."

"That is their mission in life—to keep an eye on me." Trevor bounced up and down as his virtual bike zoomed up and over a set of small hills. "I get it. They had no idea what Graham was doing. Hell, I didn't know he was doing heroin. And if I'd ever been stupid enough to take one of those pills before Graham died, I certainly wouldn't be stupid enough now."

We'd all heard that you could buy pills cheaper than beer. Something that could kill you the first time you tried it should be more expensive to warn people off. So much of my life had been out of my control; I wasn't interested in taking anything that could take control of me.

Graham had been a normal guy. One day, Trevor had walked in and found his brother taking money from their mom's purse. Money was never in short supply at their house. If Trevor asked for forty bucks, his dad handed it over, so Graham sneaking money had been strange. A month later, Trevor had found Graham dead in his car. The autopsy had said the pill he took had something besides heroin in it, which had made him stop breathing. Why in the hell would anyone want to take something that could make them stop breathing? I didn't get it.

A loud explosion came from his machine. "Well, I just crashed and burned." He climbed off his bike.

Ten seconds later, I crashed into a wall, and the game was over. "Is there any way to end this game where you don't slam into a wall?"

"Nope," Trevor said. "I think it's inevitable because it's designed that way."

"Kind of like life." I laughed.

"That's one of the things I like about you. You're so optimistic," Trevor said. "What do you want to do next?"

"Air hockey." I pointed at the machine across the room. "So now that Delia's free, maybe you should ask her out," Trevor said as we headed for the air hockey table.

"Nah. She's sister-zoned." And I just needed to remind myself of that the next time I sat across from her and her sparkly lip gloss in art class.

"Really? Because she's rocking that waitress uniform," Trevor said.

"What are you talking about?" And then I saw her. Delia had walked into Edison's and headed for the whack-a-mole game. She picked up the mallet and started whacking the crap out of the moles that popped up.

"I could be wrong," Trevor said, "but I think she's using that game as anger management."

"That's what it looks like."

"You should go talk to her. I'll go order a pizza and drinks in case she wants to join us."

"What am I supposed to say to her?" I asked.

"I'm taking care of the food," Trevor replied. "The rest is up to you."

Great. I headed over to Delia, watching as she waged war on the defenseless motorized stuffed animals. When I was within ten feet of her, she set the mallet down and turned around.

Her eyes widened, and her cheeks colored."Hello, Jack."

"Hey. Are you okay?"

"Why wouldn't I be?"

I pointed at the game. "You just whaled on the moles."

"Isn't that the point of the game?" she asked.

I stared at her for a minute.

"What?" she snapped.

"I'm trying to decide if I should offer you chocolate or duck and cover."

She leaned back against the game and crossed her arms over her chest. "I've had a strange night."

"I could take your mind off your troubles by beating you at air hockey."

"I don't like air hockey." She glanced around. "I bet I could beat you at foosball."

"Foosball is like playing with dolls on sticks."

"If you're afraid I'll beat you…"

Now she was smiling. "Let's make this interesting. If I win, you change your hair back to its normal color."

"Are you crazy? Do you know how hard it is to get this color of platinum blond?"

I rolled my eyes. "Fine, then you change your pink to a normal hair color, like brown."

"I could do that," she said, "and if I win you let me highlight your hair, or maybe give you blond tips."

"What does that mean?"

She pulled out her cell and then found a picture. "It's kind of a retro punk look. Like this."

The drummer in the photo had spiked hair, and the last half inch was blond. It was sort of cool, but I couldn't let her know I thought that. "That's ridiculous. Not that it matters, because I'm going to win."

We headed over the foosball table. She dropped the ball into play, and we both spun our men trying to get a piece of the ball. She shot it toward my goal, and I wasn't fast enough to block.

"One to nothing." She did a little dance as she announced the score, which was sort of distracting. I needed to get my head back in the game.

I managed to score two goals in a row. "Two to one," I said.

"I can count." She hit the ball. I smacked it back toward her goal. She managed to whack it so that it ricocheted into my goal. "Look at that...two to two."

We went back and forth scoring point for point until we were four for four. "This point decides who's getting a new hair color." I dropped the ball in, and Delia kicked it toward my goal. I blocked but couldn't get it clear of her first row of men. She whacked it back. I blocked again and shot it toward the side. She kicked the ball, and it slid right past my goalie.

Delia laughed and did a victory dance. "You are going to look so cool with highlights."

I dropped my head in mock defeat and then smiled back at her. "Fine. I'll let you mess with my hair, but that doesn't mean I won't wear a hat until it grows out."

"Boo," she said.

I spotted Trevor waving at me and then pointing down at the table, which must mean the food had arrived. "Trevor ordered pizza, if you want to join us."

"Thanks, but I better go. We'll talk later about when I'm going to change up your hair."

I faked confusion. "My hair? Why would we do anything to my hair?"

She snorted. "Nice try." And then she walked off.

I watched the sway of her hips until she exited the building. Was I really going to let her mess with my hair? How would that work? I imagined her running her fingers through my hair. That wouldn't be a bad thing.

Chapter Eight

DELIA

Not telling Zoe the truth about Aiden was proving difficult. "You seem oddly okay with being friend-zoned," Zoe said as we sat at her kitchen table Sunday afternoon, painting ornaments.

"Well...I guess after talking to him, I realized I still liked him as a person. It's not my fault he doesn't like me because, as we both know, I'm freaking fabulous, but I am a little bit to the left of normal, and I think he needs a quiet, kind of nerdy person to make him comfortable. The end result of this whole not quite dating mess is I can still be his friend and say things that push him outside his comfort zone, so until I find a new guy to date, I can continue to torment him. It's a win-win situation."

Zoe scrutinized me like she was waiting for me to crack and confess some secret. I had a secret, but it wasn't mine to tell. Time for evasive maneuvers.

"Would you rather I act like a drama queen and be all angry and angsty?" I asked.

"As we both know, that's my territory." Zoe set down the silver bell she'd been painting. "It's a little weird, you getting over him this quick."

"I kind of saw it coming, so I've had a while to deal with it. And truthfully, I think I'd be better off with someone more like me who doesn't give a crap about what other people think. Besides, I don't need a guy to be happy."

I grabbed the spool of gold ribbon, cut off a three-inch section, and then tied it in a bow at the top of a snowflake ornament I painted. "From my limited experience, I have found most males are a pain in the butt. So I'm not going to search for someone. I've decided it's time to let fate play itself out." I held the snowflake out for Zoe's inspection. "What do you think?"

"The hook has to go through the same spot where you tied the ribbon," Zoe said.

"It still can, but the bow makes it look nicer, and you don't have to see the paperclip holding the ornament on the tree."

"Not that I expect normal from your family, but you do realize most people use those little wire hooks to hang ornaments on their trees."

"Sorry. It's a Desmond family tradition to unbend paperclips and use those to hang our ornaments."

"Only because your mom couldn't find the hooks one year."

"And that is how fun quirky traditions are born. Plus, my mom bought Christmas-colored paper clips, so while your hooks are all a boring silver color, mine are red, gold, and green."

"I'll try not to be jealous," she said.

Jack entered the kitchen wearing blue flannel pajama pants and a gray T-shirt. That in itself wasn't abnormal. I'd seen him in his PJ's hundreds of times. What was abnormal was the fact that I noticed how the pajama pants rode low on his hips and how the T-shirt seemed to stretch tight across his shoulders. Why was I noticing his shoulders? I had no business checking out any of Jack's body parts.

"What?" Jack said right before he yawned.

"Nice bed head," I said in an attempt to cover my mental malfunction. His hair was sticking out in all directions, so neither he nor Zoe should suspect anything.

"Not like I'm looking to impress anyone," he said.

"Mission accomplished," I shot back.

He shook his head and then poured himself a glass of orange juice before heading back to the living room. The sounds of a football game blasted at top volume.

"Is your brother deaf?" I asked.

"I think he does it to keep people from talking to him," she said. "Plus he knows it annoys me."

"Jerk." Who looked hot in pajamas, I mentally added. Ugh. What was wrong with me? Just because Aiden wasn't interested didn't mean I had to latch on the closest heterosexual male.

I cut off another piece of gold ribbon and fashioned a tiny bow on the top of a Christmas tree. I held the ornament up to the light for a serious inspection. "I'm beginning to think these look like kiddy-craft projects rather than works of art."

"I painted that one," Zoe said. "So it could be my lack of artistic talent."

"It's not just the ones you did." I lined up our finished ornaments. And yes, the ones I painted did look better than Zoe's, but they still weren't up to the standard of something I'd want to represent my artistic ability. "I think I need to come up with a new idea and start over." Which seemed to be the current theme of my life.

"They may not be museum quality art, but I like them," Zoe said. "Let's finish them while you figure out another project, and I'll put them on a small tree in my room."

Why did nothing in my life seem to go the way I wanted it to? The ornaments were an insignificant bother compared to my strange new view of Jack.

...

JACK

I turned the football game on full blast so I wouldn't have to hear my sister and Delia talking non-stop. Why did girls do that? Guys didn't have to fill the silence with conversation. We only said things that needed to be said.

Delia was probably hashing and rehashing her situation with Aiden. Sometimes it seemed like girls thought if they talked or complained about something for long enough, the situation would magically change and turn into what they wanted it to be.

Just like the counselors after my dad and grandfather had died. They'd acted like talking about it would make me feel better. Wrong. I could talk for hours and they'd still be dead. What was the point? Bad things happened. That's how the world worked. No one was immune. No one was special. You just needed to enjoy what you had in your life while you had it because more than likely it would all go to crap when you least expected it.

Trevor and I had discussed my dad and grandpa and his brother a few times, but that was it. We both knew what it was like to have people ripped out of our lives before it was their time to go. It sucked. End of story.

Speaking of Trevor. I grabbed my cell and texted him. He texted me a video of Rocky lying on his side, chasing rabbits in his sleep.

My mom came into the living room, grabbed the remote, and turned down the volume. "What has you looking so happy?"

I showed her the video. She smiled. Maybe this was my chance. "Rocky's great. Do you think we could get a dog like him?"

My mom pursed her lips. "A dog is a lot of responsibility. Would you be willing to feed him, pick up the mess he leaves in the yard, and keep him clean?"

"Yes."

"Then as long as your grandmother doesn't mind, I think we can get a dog."

"Really?"

She nodded. "We'll talk about it at dinner tonight."

...

Monday morning, I met Trevor in the parking lot before school. "Guess who's getting a dog?"

"Really?" He smacked me on the shoulder. "Congratulations. Dogs make the world a better place. At least Rocky does."

"Too bad we can't clone him."

"Nope. Poor guy lost his family jewels a long time ago."

I grimaced. "Dude, I don't even like to think about that."

We walked through the parking lot, past the array of normal cars and I'm compensating for something cars. Why the snobs thought they needed a car payment the size of a house payment was beyond me. I planned to drive the Accord until the wheels fell off.

Trevor pointed at a shiny red sports car. "That thing looks like a toy. I don't know how anyone would feel safe in it."

"Don't you know?" I said. "Their dad's money forms a force field around them so they can't be hurt."

Trevor laughed.

The door to the little red car swung open, and then there were legs. Long tan legs that led up to a Wilton skirt.

"Dude." Trevor punched me. "You're drooling."

I realized I'd been staring. Not that the blond noticed. She was on her crystal-covered phone talking to someone. We held back so she'd walk in front of us.

"I want one," Trevor said.

"A fancy phone?" I said. "Because that's about the only part of that you could get."

"Wrong. I have a dog. Dogs are proven chick magnets. If I wanted to meet her, all I'd have to do was bring Rocky to school."

We slowed down and veered left, away from the crowd of girls Miss Crystal Phone was headed toward.

"I don't think she's the kind of girl who'd be okay with dog fur on her clothes."

"Her loss," Trevor said. "Besides, with the holidays coming up, I'm better off single. Having a girlfriend at Christmas is a pain in the ass. Three times I tried buying a girl the perfect gift, and each time, with each girl, I got it wrong."

"Maybe you suck at shopping," I said."Or at picking out girlfriends."

"Probably both," he agreed. "I'm not really looking forward to the holidays. My mom and dad try so hard at Christmas to pretend everything is great, like there isn't a big hole in our lives where Graham should be. I pretend everything is awesome to make them feel better."

"Yeah. The holidays suck." There was no way to ignore the gaping wound in my Christmas where my dad and grandpa should've been. We all tried to act happy for each other, but I don't think any of us liked the holidays any more. Zoe and I faked it for my mom. I was pretty sure my grandma did the same thing. Maybe this year, it wouldn't be so bad, since my mom had kind of come back to us. Maybe this year, it would only suck a little bit. That was probably the best I could hope for.

Chapter Nine

DELIA

Normally, I liked art class, but today it, or rather our, assignment annoyed me. Since Thanksgiving was this week, we were supposed to draw what we were thankful for. I sketched my parents and the box of Prismacolor pencils Aiden had given me. Which made me think of Aiden. And I was not grateful for his unsettling reveal and for what that meant for the holidays.

I'm not the type of girl who scrapbooks her fantasy wedding or fills up Pinterest with bridesmaid dresses, but given a choice, I'd rather have a boyfriend over the holidays than be single. Somehow, the holidays made being single seem like a failure, like I was somehow defective.

And unlike most people, I didn't love Thanksgiving. My parents usually volunteered to work holidays to make time and a half because it was good money. That meant I spent Thanksgiving at Zoe's which was always fun, but now all I could think of was how annoyed Jack would be.

"Do you hate that I crash your Thanksgiving every year?" I asked while I drew The Art of Tea.

Jack's arm stopped moving. He was sketching a dog. He didn't have a dog. What was up with that?

"Excuse me?"

I repeated the question and added, "Why are you drawing a dog when you don't have one?"

"First off, I've come to the inevitable conclusion that you're always going to be around on major holidays, lurking in the shadows, so I'm not offended by it. Plus, it makes it easier for me to escape and stick you and Zoe with the dishes. Second," he pointed at the drawing, "this is Rocky, Trevor's dog. I don't have a dog yet, but I'm getting one."

He didn't mind me being around for the holidays? That was a surprise. "When are you getting a dog?"

"Soon. Some time after Thanksgiving, we're going to check out the shelter."

"That's cool."

Jack pointed at my collage of sketches. "Are you really grateful for all that stuff?"

Strange question. "Yes."

"Huh." He went back to sketching.

"Why did you ask me that?"

He reached up and tugged on his tie, like the words he wanted to say wouldn't come out. "Most of the time, there isn't that much I'm thankful for."

"Because you're still mad about your dad and grandpa." The words slipped out before I thought it through.

Jack's entire body stiffened. He gripped the pencil so tight I was surprised it didn't snap in half.

Crap. I hadn't meant to offend him. Time to smooth things over. "Sorry. I didn't mean to sound so insensitive. If I were you, I'd be mad at the world, too."

The bell rang. Jack packed up his things and stomped off. Dang it. We'd been getting along, and I'd talked to him like I'd talk to Zoe, but he wasn't my friend. He may not hate me being at his house for holidays because it got him out of dish duty, but that didn't mean we were BFFs.

And of course, I was working at Betty's tonight, and odds were he was, too. Maybe I could think of something to smooth this situation over.

Between classes, I wanted to tell Zoe what I'd said but wasn't sure how she'd react. And why did I care if I'd offended Jack the Jerk? Maybe because he didn't seem like such a jerk anymore?

I had time to go home and eat something before work. When I let myself in the front door, the smell of beef stew made me drool. My mom stood in the kitchen stirring the contents of the Crock-Pot.

"Tell me that's ready to eat," I said.

"It is." She inhaled deeply. "Thank goodness for slow cookers."

"Agreed." I grabbed the ladle, filled a bowl, and sat down at the table.

"How was your day?" she asked as she fixed her own dinner.

"Mostly good. I think I said something that upset Jack."

"Zoe's brother? Since when do you two talk?"

I shrugged. "We're in art together, and we work together at Betty's. Talking seems unavoidable."

"He's turned into a hottie," my mom said.

"Mommmm, ewwww... You can't think about him like that."

"Please. Your dad was a hottie when we met in high school, so I can still spot them, even if I'm not interested in them."

"New rule. The word hottie is not part of your vocabulary."

"Fine." She grinned at me. "But you have to admit he's cute. And I can't help but notice you don't talk about Aiden anymore."

"Yeah, that didn't work out. We're better off as friends."

"Which means you'd be free to date and who knows... maybe one day you may even marry Jack. You're practically a member of the family already. Think of all the perks: no awkward getting to know the in-laws situations."

I pointed at her with my spoon. "If I didn't know where my shit-disturbing tendencies came from, you just reminded me."

"You have to admit I have a point," my mom teased.

"Nope. I don't. And I'm going to scrub that thought from my mind because...ick." I gulped down the rest of my stew and then headed upstairs to change into my retro waitress uniform. I'd just bobby pinned my tiara in place when my cell rang. It was Aiden. I let it go to voicemail because I didn't want to deal with any more drama at the moment. If he'd been my boyfriend, I would have answered, but as just a friend, I didn't feel like I owed him that kind of attention when I was getting ready for work.

After a fresh application of hot pink lip gloss with purple glitter, I was ready to act like royalty.

...

JACK

What Delia said was true, but it still pissed me off. What right did she have to talk about my dad and grandpa like what happened to them wasn't something I was supposed to be mad about? Losing both of them in the same car accident... things like that weren't supposed to happen. After they were both gone, and my mom had checked out mentally and emotionally, there didn't seem to be too much to be thankful for.

And then there was Delia filling a page with all these things she was grateful for, like her life was wonderful. How was that fair? And it's not like her life was great. Hell, she spent holidays with us because her parents volunteered to work every Thanksgiving rather than spend time with her. What did that say about her family? The more I thought about it on the drive to Betty's, the madder I got.

Hopefully, she wouldn't be working tonight.

Betty's was crowded, so I focused on checking people out and counting correct change. I saw activity over at the dessert counter, but I didn't look to see who it was.

When the sounds of someone singing "Happy Birthday" drifted through the dining room, it confirmed that Delia was working. She stood by a table full of boys who were too old to have someone sing to them. They must have done it to embarrass the kid who was having the birthday. After finishing the song, Delia set the pie on the table, said a few more words, and then headed back to the dessert case. And the birthday boy and every other guy at the table watched as she walked across the room. What the hell did they think they were doing eyeing her up that way?

"The new Pie Princess seems to be popular," Todd said from behind me.

I jumped. "Where the hell did you come from?"

"I said hello, but you were too busy glaring at the snots who were checking out the girl you claim not to like." He grinned at me.

"Shut up."

"Hey, I just came up here to invite you and anyone you might want to bring out back to the picnic table on your break. It's Vicky's birthday, and she's bringing cake and hot chocolate to celebrate."

"She's bringing cake for her own birthday?" That didn't seem right.

"I don't question things like that anymore. If it makes her happy, I just go with it. Pass the info along to Delia, would you?"

"Tell her yourself."

"Nope." He laughed and walked off.

Asshole. With no one waiting in line, I headed over to the dessert bar and passed the message to Delia.

She blinked and tilted her head. "Why is she bringing cake for her own birthday? Shouldn't he be doing something for her?"

"I don't get it, either." I reached up and scratched the back of my head. "Listen, about earlier—"

"I shouldn't have said that," Delia cut me off. "Or I shouldn't have said it that way. You have every right to be angry at the universe."

"Being mad all the time, though...it's exhausting." Wait. Why did I say that?

She moved closer, concern in her eyes. "Are you mad all the time?"

"Used to be." I shrugged. "Not so much anymore, but stupid stuff makes me angrier than I know it should. Like those jerkoffs checking you out." Son of a... Why did I say that?

She squinted. "What are you talking about?"

"The birthday table...they were..." How did I say this without sounding like I was guilty of checking her out, too? "They were staring at you in a...never mind. People doing stupid stuff set me off."

"So thinking I'm attractive is stupid?"

"What?" How had I ended up in this conversation? "No...I..."

She laughed. "Just kidding. As long as the kids aren't rude about it, I don't mind if they think I'm cute. Maybe that will translate into better tips."

A customer approached the cash register.

"I gotta go." When break time came, I headed out back. Todd and Vicky sat at a picnic table. He had one arm around her shoulders and was eating cake with the other hand. She was looking at him like just being with him in a parking lot, in the cold weather, eating cake she'd brought herself was the best thing ever.

"Happy birthday, Vicky." I sat down and grabbed a piece of cake. "So what did Todd buy you for your birthday?"

She set her fork down and held out her left hand. "The best gift ever. We're getting married."

"Holy shit." They couldn't be more than twenty or twenty-one.

"I know." Vicky grinned. "I mean, it was a given we'd get married, eventually, but I didn't expect a ring this year."

Todd shrugged. "It seemed like the right time. Plus your dad was pissed when we moved in together. This should cool his jets."

"Oh my God." Delia sat down next to me and reached for Vicky's hand. "Is that an engagement ring?"

"Isn't it gorgeous?" Vicky kissed Todd on the cheek. "He did a great job."

"Congratulations." Delia snagged a piece of cake. "You guys have been dating since you were like five, right?"

"Not quite that long, but close," Todd said.

"Falling in love with someone you've known your whole life is the best," Vicky said, "because they understand everything about you."

...

DELIA

Todd looked at Jack and then at me and raised his eyebrows. Good Lord, was he in league with my mother?

I laughed. "You are barking up the wrong tree."

Jack glanced at me. "Did I miss part of the conversation?"

"Only because you're an oblivious male," I said. "Your friend Todd here was suggesting that you and I would make a good couple."

"Nope." Jack stood and took his cake with him.

"Hey," I hollered after him. "It's not like I agree with Todd, but you don't get to be offended by the suggestion."

Jack stopped walking and turned back around. "Yes, I do. Because it's stupid, and Todd knows I think of you as an annoying little sister, and he's just doing this to piss me off." And then he turned back around and headed inside.

"Are you offended that he's offended?" Todd asked.

Am I? "Yes, because I'm the one who should get to say, 'Ewww. That's gross.' Not him."

Vicky chuckled. "You two are perfect together."

"Thanks for the cake. Happy birthday. You're insane."

I stood and stomped into the restaurant, totally irked with Todd and Vicky and their seemingly perfect relationship. Who married someone they'd fallen in love with in grade school? Honestly...it was ridiculous. No one was supposed to find their perfect match that early in life. It was annoying. I'd thought Aiden was perfect, and I'd been way off base. Heck, Aiden would probably rather kiss Jack than me. Wait, why was I thinking about anyone kissing Jack? Not that I cared. Not like I wanted to kiss Jack. Just because he'd somehow turned into a hottie when I wasn't paying attention didn't mean he was boyfriend material.

As I walked by him, he muttered something under his breath. I didn't stop to see what he was griping about because a woman was standing at the dessert case eyeing up the pecan pie. I slid behind the glass case and slipped into my Pie Princess persona.

"Can I help you?"

The woman tapped the glass counter with her French manicure that was chipping off on the ends. Probably because she used her nails like a jackhammer. "I want a piece of that pecan pie."

I reached into the case and pulled out a pie, which I'd already cut into individual pieces. "Would you like that for here or boxed up to go?"

"I don't want that pie." The woman pointed at the perfectly good pie I held. "I want a piece of that pie." Again she tapped the counter and a bit of her white nail tip flaked off.

I knew the mantra that the customer was always right, but Betty had impressed upon me that we only cut up one pie at a time. Otherwise some pieces could go to waste. I didn't think that was a possibility, because if she ever tried to throw out pie, I'm sure whoever was nearby would volunteer to eat the remaining pieces rather than let them land in the trash.

Maybe the woman would be reasonable. "They are both pecan pies, ma'am. And this one is already cut, so I'm supposed to serve it first."

"I don't want that one." The woman's voice carried across the room. Several diners and Jack glanced over to see what was going on.

Crap. Decision time. Did I give in and send the woman on her way with the specific piece of pie she wanted or stick to the rules I'd been given?

Someone approached in my peripheral vision. "Mrs. Banks, is there a problem?" Jack asked.

"This young lady won't sell me a piece of pie."

What the heck? I held up the pie, which was already cut into pieces. "Betty told me not to cut another pie until this one is gone."

"Mrs. Banks has been eating here since the restaurant opened," Jack said. "So you should just give her the pie she wants, because she won't change her mind."

"No, I won't." The woman beamed at Jack. "You're always such a helpful young man."

I bit my tongue, kept my rant to myself, and cut into the new pie, giving Mrs. Banks what she wanted. I even tied a pretty ribbon around the box, making sure the knot was extra tight. My version of being passive-aggressive.

The woman paid for the pie and headed for the front door. When she was out of earshot, I turned to Jack. "What in the heck was that about?"

He smiled like he was in on a joke I didn't understand. "Mrs. Banks once waited an hour for the specific table she wanted, rather than sitting at one of the other open tables. I think she prides herself on being difficult. You can't reason with her. It's best just to give her what she wants."

I took a deep breath and blew it out. "I hate people who think they should be treated differently than everyone else. Like they get some pass on the standard rules because they're better in some weird way."

He shrugged. "She's not worth getting upset over."

"I thought you were the king of being angry at everything." Crap. I really needed to reinstall that filter on my mouth.

Instead of stomping off, Jack chuckled. "It's all a matter of perspective. Eccentric old ladies don't make me mad, but old men who call me son—they tick me off."

Chapter Ten

JACK

I blinked. Why did I tell her that?

Delia tilted her head and studied me. The light reflected off her sparkling pink lip gloss. "You didn't mean to say that, did you?"

"No."

"You can, though...share stuff with me, I mean. Like we said before, I am practically family."

Family. Right. Family who wore distracting sparkly lip goo. "I better get back to the cash register."

"Thanks for helping," Delia called out after me.

I waved as I walked away. As I rang out customers, I kept my eyes straight ahead rather than check out Delia as she sold pie. When my shift ended, she was already gone.

In the parking lot, I saw Delia sitting in her truck. I climbed in my car and started the ignition, waiting to see what she was doing. Exhaust came out of her tailpipe, so she wasn't having car problems or truck problems, or however you'd say that. She was texting someone. Maybe that Aiden guy.

Whatever. None of my business who she texted. Just because we were being civil to one another didn't mean I needed to babysit her in the parking lot. There were plenty of people in Delia's life who'd help her if she needed something. It's not like I was special.

...

The smell of turkey hit me when I walked in the front door. My grandmother stood in the kitchen stirring a pot on the stove. "What are you making?" Thanksgiving was three days away. She couldn't be baking the turkey now.

"It takes all day for the turkey to bake in the roaster, and the smell always makes me want turkey soup. This year I thought I'd cheat the system by having turkey soup ready ahead of time." She dipped a spoon in the pot and tasted it. "It's done. Do you want some?"

"Sure." I joined her in the kitchen and accepted the bowl she ladled out for me. "Where are Mom and Zoe?"

"They went Christmas shopping."

I tried the soup. "It's good."

"Of course it is." She grinned. "Anything you want to talk about since we have the house to ourselves for a little bit?"

I thought about it. "Not really."

"Are you bringing anyone to Thanksgiving?"

"Not unless Trevor wants to stop by. How about you?"

My grandmother had been dating this Everett guy, who happened to be Zoe's boyfriend's grandpa.

"I enjoy Everett's company, but holidays are for family."

"And apparently Delia," I muttered. "Why doesn't her family ever have their own Thanksgiving?"

"Delia's mom isn't really a cook, and I think the money is too good for them to pass up. Do you mind Delia being here?"

"I'm used to it, but I kind of feel sorry for her. If you and Mom decided you'd rather work for extra money instead of having Thanksgiving, I'd be mad."

"Maybe since she's never really known anything different, it seems normal."

...

Thanksgiving morning, I woke up to the sound of people talking in the kitchen, courtesy of the heating vent. I grabbed my cell off the nightstand and checked the time. Nine. At least I'd slept in a little bit. I lay there a minute to eavesdrop on the conversation before going downstairs, because sometimes it was good to know what I was walking into.

"Grant said Aiden wanted to ask you to come by his house for Thanksgiving." That was Zoe's voice. She must be talking to Delia. Was Delia already over here, or were they on the phone?

"Why would I do that?" Delia said.

Crap. She was already here. No Delia-free time for me today.

"I already have a friend to spend Thanksgiving with—you. Why would I want to spend it with him?" Delia sounded annoyed. Apparently, she wasn't over this stupid Aiden guy, not that I cared who she dated. It was none of my business.

"Maybe he's reconsidering your relationship," Zoe said.

"Nope. Been there. Done that. He chose the sucky ending, and he gets to live with it."

My life would be easier if she was off the market. I rubbed my eyes, trying to erase the images from my dream last night where Delia and I had been way more than friends. And it had seemed so real. She'd had a flat tire after work, so I'd given her a ride home. She'd asked me to come in since no one was home to check out the house. How often did she go home to an empty house? That would kind of suck. Being down two family members was bad, but not having anyone in the house would be worse.

Anyway, I'd checked the house, and then when I went to leave, my car wouldn't start, and it had started to sleet, so I decided to camp out at her house on the sofa. It was like my brain was coming up with reasons to push us together, and it had worked. Her sparkly lip gloss had tasted like watermelon Jolly Ranchers. I scratched my head. Had I ever dreamed a taste before? Not that I could remember.

My cell beeped. A text from Trevor showed Rocky with some weird plastic thing around his neck. It took a minute to realize it was the swinging lid to a trash can. I laughed. He must have stuck his head in the trash can to steal something and ended up with the lid stuck around his neck. I texted back, Not sure the new collar is a good look for him.

Trevor texted back a quick LOL.

My stomach growled. Time for breakfast.

...

DELIA

Why would Aiden think I'd want to spend Thanksgiving with him? Did he just want to use me as a fake girlfriend to make peace with his father? Not that I could blame him. I wasn't ready to be that good of a friend yet. Rational or not, it still stung I wasn't his type.

"Look," Zoe said.

I tuned back into reality and glanced in the direction she pointed. Fat, white snowflakes swirled through the air, obstructing the view out the kitchen window. "Were we supposed to have snow today?"

"The weather report said a chance of flurries." Zoe's grandmother mixed together the cream of mushroom soup and green beans for a casserole. "I think they may have underestimated."

Jack entered the kitchen wearing Minion pajama bottoms and a navy T-shirt. I'd hoped finding him attractive in his PJ's would be a one time aberration. Nope. He was sleep rumpled and adorable and hot, and that was just wrong.

"Are you going to complain about my bed head again?" Jack asked.

"No. And speaking of—I haven't forgotten that you lost that bet." Come on, brain, think of something else to say. I pointed at his pants. "But I never figured you for Minion pajamas."

He shrugged. "I think they were my white elephant gift last year."

"I won those," Zoe said, "but they were too big for me, so I gave them to Jack."

"That's right," Jack said. "I offered you my Chia cat, but you weren't interested."

"Those things are creepy," I said. "My grandma used to grow them on her kitchen windowsill. They gave me nightmares."

"You're afraid of Chia pets?" Jack laughed. "Here I thought you were this kick-ass girl who wasn't afraid of anything."

Jack thought I was kick-ass? Since when? "Normally, I am a superhero, but those Chia-things are freaky. It didn't help that my grandmother painted faces on the animals, and she always gave them mean eyes and pointed teeth."

"I used to be scared of your grandma." Jack poured himself a bowl of cereal.

"Join the club," Zoe said.

"She was a little intense," I said.

Jack took his cereal into the living room.

"You and Jack seem to be getting along better," Zoe's grandma said.

I froze for a second and then went with, "He's a pretty decent guy as long as Zoe and I don't interrupt his naps."

"Why don't you girls get started on the pumpkin bread?"

"Sure." Zoe stood up and went to gather ingredients. Technically, I didn't need to come over this early, but sitting in my empty house, which on a normal day didn't bother me, felt lonely on Thanksgiving. I'd never say anything to my parents, but I didn't understand why they continued to work all the holidays. When I was younger, I knew they'd needed the money. And it's not like we'd become rich since then, but we were comfortable, or at least that's how I saw it. Broken-down appliances aside, I didn't understand why they never made the effort for us to spend time together on special days.

My cell beeped. I checked text messages. My mom needed me to run back home and make sure she'd plugged in the Crock-Pot or she and my dad wouldn't have anything to eat when they came home tonight. I showed the message to Zoe. "Looks like I have an errand to run."

"Want me to go with you?" Zoe asked.

"Nah, stay and make the pumpkin bread. I'll be right back."

I grabbed my coat and scarf, making sure to zip my coat all the way up before heading out the door. The air had a cold metallic smell I associated with winter. The snow was starting to add up. It looked like we had an inch or more already.

My old truck was pretty good in the snow, so I wasn't worried. As I drove to my house, the peaceful fat snowflakes disappeared and were replaced by the ping of sleet hitting the roof. Crap. I hated sleet. Snow was pretty and magical. Sleet was scary and ugly. I slowed down and put on my brights. If some idiot came barreling from the other direction on this two-lane back road, I wanted him to see my truck so he wouldn't hit me.

My cell beeped, but I didn't stop to check it. Driving in bad weather wasn't my favorite thing to do. But I'd hate for my mom and dad to come home to a meal of Pop-Tarts on Thanksgiving. The drive to my house took twice as long as it should.

The sleet and snow mixture created a sheet of ice that coated the trees and my driveway. I parked right up next to the house, hoping to avoid some of the sleet. I'd just run in and turn the Crock-Pot on and then dash back out. Hopefully, the ice wouldn't have time to build up on my truck.

I stepped out of the truck, carefully planting one foot and then the other. The driveway was slick. Holding onto the truck, I wobbled my way around the front end and across the sidewalk toward the front door.

The porch steps were slippery. I should probably salt them before I went back to Zoe's. In the kitchen, I found the Crock-Pot, full of ingredients with the cord dangling off the counter. I plugged it in and texted my mom, Mission accomplished.

She texted back a smiley face. I went to the pantry to find rock salt for the steps. Half a bag sat next to the flashlights and the wind-up radio my dad had purchased for when the power went out.

I filled up the coffee can we kept in the bag and carried it back out the front door with me. I sprinkled the salt as I slipped and slid my way back to the truck. If the weather continued like this, I'd probably stay the night at Zoe's.

...

JACK

I was salting the front porch when Delia drove up the driveway and parked. Her entire truck was coated with ice. Why had she gone out in this? She opened the driver's side door and climbed out in slow motion.

"Are you okay?" I called out.

"Just trying not to fall." She made her way to the front steps and latched onto the banister.

"I salted those, but they might still be slippery," I warned.

"I hate this ice crap. Snow is pretty. This stuff sucks."

"Agreed."

She made it to the porch without falling down. "Good job."

"Thanks, I try." She headed for the door, and then she flailed as her feet went out from under her, and she tilted backward like she was going to fall down the steps.

I dropped the rock salt and grabbed her, yanking her hard toward me to keep her from tumbling backward. She hit my chest with a thump and a few muttered curse words.

She looked up at me, her brown eyes huge. "Thank you."

It didn't seem like she was in a hurry to move away from me. Holding her like this felt oddly comfortable. I realized if I leaned down just a little bit, I'd be in the perfect position to kiss her. Wait. Where did that thought coming from? I needed to snap back to reality. "Are you all right?" I loosened my grip but didn't let go.

"Yes." She gave a nervous laugh and moved back a step, holding onto my arm. "That was one of those life flashing in front of my eyes moments."

"What's going on?" Zoe said from the front door.

"Delia tried to do a backward dive off the porch." I moved toward the doorway, bringing Delia with me and letting her go once she reached the welcome mat.

"I can't believe how slippery it's gotten." Delia released my arm and went into the house. She glanced back at me, her cheeks red. "Thanks again."

I nodded and went back to flinging salt on the porch and steps. Once I was done, I headed into the kitchen, where my mom was making hot tea.

"Want a cup?" she asked me.

"Yes." I inhaled the smell of fresh pumpkin bread. "Tell me the pumpkin bread is done."

"I went with pumpkin muffins." Zoe pointed at the muffins still in the tin on the stove. "But yes, they're done, and they should be cool enough to eat."

I picked the biggest muffin in the tin and took the cup of hot tea my mom offered me. "I can't believe how slick it's gotten out there."

"I hate to think of my parents driving in this weather," Delia said.

"Do you know where they went today?" Zoe asked.

"I think my dad's in town, but my mom was driving to a couple of nursing homes that aren't close."

Worrying about people getting into car accidents was now one of my family's special skill sets. I wasn't going to lie and tell Delia her parents were going to be fine, because who knew if that was the truth? Maybe I could distract her. "What's the deal with those ornaments you've been painting?" I asked.

"I was going to sell them at the Christmas Flea Market, but they didn't turn out like I wanted them to."

"You could draw people's portraits or make them into caricatures like they do at the carnivals," I suggested.

"That's a great idea," Delia said. "I could just take some supplies and post a few examples of my work."

"And while they're having their picture drawn, I can tempt them with homemade Christmas cookies," Zoe said.

I noticed my mom and grandma were smiling at each other like they'd done something sneaky. "What?"

"Nothing," my mom said. "I'm just glad to see all three of you in the same room, having a civil conversation."

"I think the separate car idea really did help your relationship," my grandmother said.

Personally, I thought it had more to do with Delia and her sparkly lip gloss, but I nodded like I agreed.

"I think working together at Betty's helped, too," Delia said. "I was able to see Jack as a person rather than as Zoe's brother."

That didn't make much sense. "I'm still Zoe's brother."

"I know, but you're multidimensional now instead of being slotted into one flat category."

"How can a category be flat?" I asked, just to annoy her.

"It's an analogy that works in your favor," Delia said. "Just go with it."

"Fine." I grinned and drank my tea.

The timer on the oven beeped. My grandmother grabbed her oven mitts. "I believe it's turkey time."

My mom scooted away from the oven to give my grandmother some room. She was smiling. I glanced around and realized everyone in the kitchen looked happy. Maybe our holidays weren't doomed to be sad forever.

Chapter Eleven

DELIA

Sitting at Zoe's kitchen table, I stared at what was left of Thanksgiving dinner on my plate. There wasn't much...a single green beans and few crumbs from my dinner roll. I groaned and wrapped my arms around my waist. "I'm never eating again."

"We haven't had pie yet," Zoe reminded me.

I pushed my chair away from the table. "I have to take a break, maybe walk around a bit, before I eat pie."

"You're assuming there'll be pie left when you come back," she said.

"That's just mean." I picked up my plate and carried it to the sink. Everyone else still sat at the table. "Want me to make coffee?"

"Yes," Zoe's grandma said. "Pie without coffee is just wrong."

"Pumpkin pie without whipped cream is wrong," I replied.

"It's already made up and in the fridge," Zoe said.

I peeled a new paper coffee filter from the stack inside the cabinet and added it to the coffeemaker. Then I dumped in the coffee grounds, eyeballing the amount.

"You're supposed to use eight tablespoons," said Jack.

"That's the boring way to make coffee," I replied.

I pushed the button and waited to hear the sound of coffee percolating and dripping into the carafe. Nothing happened.

"It helps if you add water," Zoe called out.

Right. "I blame the turkey. It's putting me to sleep." I filled the water reservoir and then yawned and leaned against the counter. "I'll just nap until it's done." I was only half kidding. I swear I'd eaten my weight in turkey and stuffing and homemade macaroni and cheese.

When the coffeemaker stopped making noises, I opened my eyes. "Who wants a cup?" There was a chorus of "me's" from the kitchen table, so I grabbed five mugs and poured. Then I grabbed two mugs in each hand and delivered them to the table before going back for my own coffee and the whipped cream. There was a slice of pie waiting on my place mat when I returned. I added a giant glob of whipped cream to my plate.

"You sure that's enough?" Jack asked.

"I like a two-to-one whipped cream to pie ratio." I passed the bowl of whipped cream and dug in.

I listened as Zoe and her family talked about different things, content to eat my pie and observe. They may have lost two members, but they were more a family than mine ever was. Jack smiled and laughed, which I hadn't seen him do much lately. It looked good on him. Earlier when he'd grabbed me on the steps to keep me from falling and held onto me for a moment, it had felt right, which was frightening.

My cell buzzed. I checked the text, and my stomach sank. "What's wrong?" Jack asked.

"My mom says it's gotten so bad out that she plans to stay at a motel rather than trying to drive home when she finishes her shift. On a positive note, the motel is attached to a diner, so she can still have Thanksgiving dinner."

"What about your dad?" Zoe asked.

"Mom said his shift ends in a few hours, and he plans to drive home and enjoy turkey tetrazzini for one from the Crock-Pot."

"He's welcome to join us," Zoe's mom said. "And it goes without saying that you're staying the night."

"Thanks. I planned on it. I'll call him and see if he wants to come over." I stood and walked into the living room to make the call.

"Hey, Delia. Tell me you're safe and sound at Zoe's," my dad said by way of a greeting.

"Hello to you, too, and yes, I am. You're invited to come over here for dinner later if you want."

"Tell Zoe's family I appreciate the offer, but I decided to pick up some extra hours since no one else wants to get out in this weather."

"You're not driving anywhere, are you?"

"Nope. I'm staying right where I'm at. I may sleep an hour or two in the on-call room before I come home."

That sounded like a lonely way to spend the holiday. "Maybe next Thanksgiving, we could all stay home together or all come over here?"

"As long as no major appliances commit suicide, I think that might be a good idea." He sighed. "I never used to mind working the holidays, but this weather has made me reconsider."

Disappointment turned my stomach, or maybe it was that last bite of pie. It might be immature, but I wanted him to want to stay home to have a family dinner, not because of the sucky weather.

"I'll see you tomorrow, sweetheart," Dad said.

"Sure. I'll bring home some leftovers." I hung up and went to stare out the living room window. Sleet coated the trees and my truck, giving everything an odd glass-like appearance.

Zoe joined me. "Everything okay?"

I nodded. "They're both safe."

Zoe's cell buzzed, she checked the screen, and her face lit up, which could mean only one thing.

"It's Grant," Zoe said and then zipped across the room and up the stairs.

Mentally, I rolled my eyes. While I was happy that Zoe was so in love, it sucked that my own romantic life was nonexistent.

Jack exited the kitchen and stopped next to me to peer out the window. "The ice is cool in a creepy sort of way."

"As long as you don't have to drive in it." Something moved out in the yard and then ran under my truck. "What was that?"

Jack moved closer to the window, exhaled, and fogged up the glass. He wiped the condensation away with his sleeve. "Is that a rabbit? Why isn't it hunkered down in a burrow somewhere?"

"Maybe it's a baby, and it's lost." I walked over and grabbed my coat off the hook where I'd hung it to dry. Jack must have had the same idea, because he grabbed his coat at the same time.

"You're not going out there," he said.

I laughed."I'm going to go with the childish, yet effective, 'You're not the boss of me' line."

"If you fall, who's going to catch you while I'm trying to scoop up a half-frozen rabbit?"

He made a good point, but I wasn't going to let that stop me. "We'll both go out there. I'll stand on the porch and hold a box that you can put the rabbit in after you catch it."

"Okay." He walked back into the kitchen and returned with a plastic storage container with a towel inside.

"What do you think you're doing with my good tea towel?" Jack's mom asked.

"Rescue operation," I said. "For a small furry creature hiding under my truck."

"Wait," his mom said. She went to the bathroom and returned with a bath towel that was frayed on the edges. "Use this instead, and be careful."

I opened the door and tested my footing on the doormat. Not too bad. I put my left hand on the wall and held the box in my right hand. Once I'd cleared the doorway, Jack came out, taking slow measured steps to the porch stairs. He grasped the railing with his gloved hand; when his foot hit the first step, he flailed and latched onto the railing with his other hand.

"Careful," I called out.

He snorted. "I'm working on it." Once he made it down the front steps, he skated over to my truck and crouched down. He reached under, and something whined.

"I'm not going to hurt you." Jack pulled out something covered in brown fur and held it to his chest. "I've got you." He took smaller steps coming back to the house like he was making the effort to be more careful.

"Bring the box to the edge of the stairs so I can pass this little guy off to you."

Doing as he asked, I inched my way forward and grabbed the railing, squatting down and holding out the box so he could reach up and put the animal inside.

He set a small furry critter in the box. "I think it's a puppy."

Whatever it was, it was shivering like crazy. It's eyes were matted shut with frost. "Poor little guy." I folded the towel over him and then waited for Jack to join me on the porch. "You carry him," I said. "I don't want to fall and hurt him."

"We got this." Jack put his arm around my lower back. "You hold him, and I'll hold you."

Warmth blossomed in my chest. I had no idea Jack was such a good guy.

...

JACK

I held on to Delia as we made our way back into the house. Once we cleared the doorway, I let go, pulled off my gloves, unzipped my coat, and picked up the frozen pup, holding him against my chest. "I hope we aren't too late."

"Is it a rabbit?" my mom asked.

"A puppy," I said.

"Let me put a towel in the dryer to warm it up." My mom hurried down the hall.

"Is he okay?" Delia asked.

"I can feel him breathing."

Delia placed her fingers on the towel-covered puppy, the rest of her hand against my chest.

"What are you doing?" Zoe said as she came down the stairs.

"Puppy rescue," Delia said and then filled Zoe in on the details.

My mom came back with the warm towel. "Why don't you sit on the couch?"

I unwrapped the puppy and transferred him to the warm towel. "Hey, little guy." His eyes were open now, and he wasn't shivering as hard. Bits of ice were clumped in his brown fur. I bundled him up and held him. He was about the same size as a football. He looked at me and whined. "Don't worry, buddy. You're safe."

"What kind of dog do you think he is?" Delia asked.

"Can't tell," my mom said. "He isn't wearing a collar."

She reached out and petted the exposed portion of his head. "Jack, you may have gotten an early Christmas present."

"What are you going to call him?" Delia asked.

I thought about it. "Buddy seems right."

"I like it," Delia said. "And since I helped rescue him, I want visitation rights."

"Like you're not over here all the time anyway," I said.

"Now I'll just have to come over even more." She grinned and leaned close so she could peek at Buddy. "I think he's sleeping."

Small snoring sounds drifted up from the towel. A sweet scent, like cake, drifted up from Delia's hair. For the moment, all seemed right with the world.

"Delia, why don't we Google what you should feed puppies when you don't have dog food?" Zoe said.

"Good idea." Delia hopped up and wandered off with Zoe. For a moment there, it had felt like Delia and I were a team, and then Zoe had yanked her away. But that was okay. I didn't need to think about girls, because I had a dog. His soft snoring sounds made me smile.

Zoe came back carrying a small tray with a bowl of water and a plate of sweet potatoes and turkey.

"The turkey I understand, but sweet potatoes?"

"We rinsed the turkey to wash off some of the seasoning, and we baked the sweet potato in the microwave. Apparently, dogs love them."

Buddy wriggled against my chest. "I think the smell woke him up."

"Where should we feed him?" Zoe asked.

"Kitchen," I said, "because that's where he'll normally eat."

Zoe put the food on the floor by the side of the refrigerator, and I set Buddy down next to the tray. His fur was wet but not frozen. He made quick work of the food and sampled the water. Then he turned in a circle and lay down on the towel.

"I guess he's worn out." Delia reached for him but stopped. "Can I hold him?"

"Sure."

Buddy became the most popular person in the house that night as everyone asked to hold him. It was kind of cool the way they acted like he was mine. I expected Zoe to run off with him, but she didn't.

Chapter Twelve

JACK

That night, Buddy slept in my bed. In the middle of the night, I woke to him whining and standing at the edge of the mattress. When I put him down, he ran to the door. It took me a minute to realize he needed to go out.

Great. How could I do this in the ice? Maybe he could just go on the porch and I'd clean it up in the morning, because I wasn't going down those porch steps if I didn't need to.

I opened the front door and set him on the doormat, where he did his business and then ran back into the house, looking at me like I might try to make him go back outside. "We'll figure this out in the morning." I shoved the doormat over a foot so anyone stepping out the door wouldn't land in the small steaming pile of dog doo and then took Buddy back up to bed. He was a smart guy. Had he belonged to someone and gotten lost in the ice storm? My heart sank at the thought. If he'd been someone's pet, he would've had on a collar, right? And not to be a jerk, but barring extenuating circumstances, anyone who let their dog wander off in an ice storm didn't necessarily deserve to get him back.

In the upstairs hall, Delia came toward me wearing Wonder Woman pajamas. "Is Buddy okay?" she asked.

"He needed to go out. Why are you awake?"

"I woke up from the weirdest nightmare about my house falling apart around me." She shook her head. "It sounds stupid, but it was scary, and it seemed so real. I'm not ready to go back to sleep. I thought pumpkin pie would make me feel better."

"Can't hurt." I felt oddly awake. "I think Buddy and I will join you."

She smiled and reached to pet Buddy. Her fingers grazed my chest as she scratched his ears. "He's so cute."

I wished she'd look at me the way she looked at Buddy.

...

DELIA

Sitting in the kitchen with Jack and Buddy while everyone else in the house slept made it feel like we were having some sort of secret relationship. Not that I wanted a relationship with Jack. So what if he saved puppies from ice storms and caught me when I was about to fall? Any guy would do those things, right? Probably not, and they probably wouldn't look so cute with their hair sticking out all over.

There was one section of hair standing almost straight up on top of his head, like half of a Mohawk. "I have to fix this." I reached over and ran my fingers through his hair a couple of time, flattening out the section. His hair was softer than I thought it would be.

Jack was looking at me like he was confused about something.

"What?"

His gaze dropped to my mouth for a second, and then he glanced back up. The air between us felt charged, like if he touched me I'd be zapped with static electricity.

I suddenly became aware of how close we were sitting next to each other. Earlier, he'd pulled his chair over to mine so I could hold Buddy while he ate, and he'd never scooted back. And I'd been totally comfortable with the proximity, just like on the porch when he'd caught me and held me in his arms for a moment.

If he were anyone but Zoe's brother, I would have leaned toward him, encouraging a kiss. What would he do if I leaned in right now, closing the distance between our mouths?

Buddy barked, startling me and breaking the spell. I looked down at the little guy. "What was that for?"

He wagged his tail at me and put his paws on the table. "I don't know if you can have pumpkin pie."

He whined.

Jack scooted his chair back and stood. "I'll make him some food."

I avoided eye contact with Jack, afraid he'd somehow know what I'd been thinking. Once Buddy's food was ready, I set him down on the floor so he could eat, put my dirty dishes in the sink, and faked a yawn. "Thanks for keeping me company. I think I can go back to sleep now."

"Night," he said.

Apparently, I was the only one experiencing inner turmoil, which sort of sucked. "Night." I padded off across the floor and back upstairs.

When I woke up the next morning, Zoe was nowhere to be seen. She must have gotten up and decided to let me sleep. I checked my cell. It was nine thirty.

Since I'd eaten pie at two in the morning, I wasn't hungry for breakfast, so I took a quick shower and found some of my clothes in Zoe's closet. It really was like I lived here. Over the years, I'd left clothes here on accident, and Zoe's mom had always just washed them and hung them in Zoe's closet. It was such a blessing to have Zoe and her family in my life. Without them, I'd be sitting at home on the holidays and most evenings, watching television by myself. And that was the reason I had to stop daydreaming about kissing Jack. If by some weird twist of fate, he liked me, too, and we started dating, eventually we'd break up, and then I'd lose everything—no more Thanksgiving, or Christmas, or girls' trips to the nail salon.

Why was I worrying about something that would never happen?

In the kitchen, I drank a cup of coffee and talked with Zoe about Grant. Jack sat in the living room holding Buddy while watching football at a surprisingly reasonable volume.

"It doesn't look so bad outside," Zoe's grandmother said.

I popped up and looked out the kitchen window above the sink. "It looks like the ice melted off my truck. That's a good sign. Do you mind if I pack some leftovers for my mom and dad?"

"Of course not," Zoe's mom said.

"You know, I really appreciate you guys being here for me all the time." Why did it feel like I was about to cry?

"We love having you here." Zoe's mom gave me a quick hug. "Hopefully, next year your parents will be smart enough to come with you."

I packed up some food, said my good-byes in the kitchen, and then stopped to see Buddy on the way out, which meant I also stopped to talk to Jack.

"See you later." I rubbed Buddy's ears. "You, too," I told Jack as I walked away. He grunted in response.

The drive home was fine. The ice had melted, leaving slushy puddles and ugly gray snow. When I pulled up my driveway, I was surprised to see both my parents' cars. Even if they were there, that didn't mean they were available. More than likely, they were both sleeping.

I used my key to open the front door and heard the sound of laughter coming from the kitchen, and the house smelled like cinnamon rolls. Curious, I investigated.

"Good morning." My mom saluted me with her cup of coffee. "We were hoping you'd be home soon."

"Really? Why?"

"I told your mom what you said about us spending Thanksgiving together as a family. We'll try to make that happen next year, but for now, we're starting a new tradition called Family Friday. Your mom is going to cook, which could be scary." Then he pointed at the table where Monopoly and Clue were stacked with some other games. "We can play games or watch movies or do whatever you want, as long as we do it as a family."

It felt like an empty space in my chest filled up with warmth. "That sounds wonderful. And if whatever Mom cooks doesn't turn out, I brought home leftovers."

"I would be offended, but I'm hoping you brought home stuffing. I can make the box kind, but it doesn't compare to Zoe's grandma's."

I set the bag of Ziploc containers on the table. "No, it doesn't, and yes, I did."

"Then let Family Fun Day begin." My mom pointed at the oven. "Do you want to check on the cinnamon rolls?"

"Sure." I grabbed a pot holder and opened the oven door. The popcorn pan contained what looked like two tubes of Pillsbury Cinnamon rolls. "It smells good." I pulled the pan out and put it on the stove top. "The most important question is where is the icing?"

"On top of the microwave for safekeeping," my dad said. "And we made two batches so we'd have more icing per roll if you want."

"I like how you think." I slathered icing on half the rolls.

"I think there's canned frosting in the pantry if we need more," my mom said. "I'll pour the milk."

For the first time in months, we ate together and played games while watching It's a Wonderful Life. And at the moment, it was.

...

JACK

All weekend I worried about someone knocking on our door asking about a lost dog. At this point, unless it was a little girl crying over her lost pet, I was ready to lie and claim I'd picked Buddy up from the shelter. He was content to sit on my lap when I watched television. He was too small to chase a tennis ball, so Zoe had come up with the idea of balling up a clean sock so he could chase that, which turned into a game of tug-of-war.

"You should make an appointment at the vet," my grandma said. "Just to make sure he's okay."

Buddy growled as he pulled on the now stretched-out sock. "He looks healthy." I slowly let the sock slip from my grasp like Buddy had yanked it from my hand. He did a doggy victory trot around the room and then brought the sock back to me to start the game again.

"We want him to stay that way. I can take him while you're at school tomorrow."

Stupid as it may sound, the thought of leaving Buddy and going to school made me nervous. "I wonder if I could sneak him into school in my backpack."

"He'd fit," my grandmother said. "But I don't think he'd be happy about it."

"I know." I hated to let him out of my sight. Good things had a way of disappearing from my life.

"Don't worry," my grandmother said. "I'll keep a close watch on him while you're at school."

"If someone shows up looking for him, promise me you won't give him away without me having a chance to say good-bye."

"I don't think you have to worry about that. If anyone was looking for him, they would have come around asking about him already."

A knock sounded on the door. The timing was ominous. "I'll get that," my grandmother said.

Having a bad feeling about this, I picked up Buddy and carried him to the kitchen, where I could eavesdrop but no one could see us. A guy in a leather motorcycle jacket stood in the doorway with a boy who looked like he was in seventh grade.

"Good morning. I was wondering if you found a puppy around here?"

Shit.

Buddy chose that moment to start wriggling and barking. Taking a deep breath, I walked over where they could see me. "We found Buddy."

The man smiled. "We called him Brownie."

Double shit.

The kid walked into the house and held out his hands. "Is he okay?"

Against every instinct, I held Buddy out to him. "See for yourself."

He took Buddy and hugged him. "I'm so sorry. I thought you'd be safe in the shed."

"What happened?" I asked.

The kid's dad said, "We kept a litter of pups in the shed, not realizing the ice storm was going to hit. I think the sound of it made some of the puppies run away. I'm glad he's okay. He's the only one we hadn't tracked down."

"He's a good dog." I swallowed over the lump in my throat and backed up a step, trying to put some distance between myself and Buddy. I should have known better than to become attached.

"You want to keep him?" the dad asked.

"Yes," I blurted out.

The boy kissed Buddy and passed him back to me. "He was my favorite of the bunch. You'll take good care of him, right?"

I held Buddy and looked into his soulful brown eyes.

"Yes."

"I'm glad this had a happy ending," the man said. "I was scared he didn't make it."

"We'll give him a good home," my grandmother reassured the man. "What kind of dog is he?"

The man smiled. "Our dogs are both rescues. Near as we can tell, his mom is a beagle-border collie mix, and his dad is a chocolate lab-hound mix. So he's not going to stay little for long."

"I thought his feet looked big," my grandma said.

We all said our good-byes, and then I took Buddy over to the couch and sat down. He was mine now. Really mine.

My grandmother sat next to me and put her arm around my shoulders. "Just so you know, I was prepared to arm wrestle that man for Buddy."

I laughed. "With those muscles you built up crocheting all the time, you probably could've taken him."

...

DELIA

Family Friday had been amazing. Now it was back to the normal school and work week, which meant I heard my parents leave in the middle of the night, and they were sometimes home before I left to go to work at Betty's. I ate dinner alone every night and went to bed alone, and of course, I had Zoe to hang out with, and I could have stayed over at her house, but the general rule had always been we avoided sleepovers on school nights, if at all possible. Because even though it sometimes felt like I lived at Zoe's house, I didn't actually live at Zoe's house.

Friday, on the drive home from school, my truck started pulling to the right. What was that about? By the time I made it into the driveway, I knew it had to be one of the tires. Sure enough, when I investigated, the right front tire was almost flat.

No other cars in the driveway meant my dad wasn't home. And yes, I knew how to change a flat tire, but it was twenty-two degrees outside, and I didn't want to do it, damn it. I'm not the damsel-in-distress type, but every once in a while, it would be nice to have someone who could step in and fix things. A guy who would take care of me because he thought I was special and he liked doing nice things for me. Of course, that guy only existed in the fantasyland of my imagination.

I stomped into the house and checked the time. I was due at Betty's in an hour. First, I texted my dad. He answered right away, telling me not to mess with the tire. He'd take care of it when he came home. Thank God. Problem number one taken care of.

On to problem number two. How would I get to work? If Jack was working, maybe he could give me a ride. Problem number three...I didn't know Jack's cell number, so I texted Zoe. She texted back, offering to give me a ride to work if Jack wasn't able to, and she gave me his number.

I texted him.

My cell rang. "Do you want me to look at your tire before work?" Jack asked.

Wow. That was nice of him. "Thanks for offering, but my dad said he'd take care of it when he comes home, so I just need a ride."

"I'll pick you up in forty minutes."

"Thanks." Okay. Crisis averted. Now what? I changed for work and ate some Pop-Tarts, because there wasn't much else in the house. I'd have to order some carry-out from Betty's so there'd be food when my parents came home.

Jack honked when he pulled up to my house. I slipped my coat on and jogged out the front door. It was snowing again, which made me think of Buddy.

I grabbed the passenger door handle of the Honda Accord and pulled. Nothing happened.

"Sorry," Jack said from inside the car, and then I heard the click of the automatic unlock button.

I tried again, and this time it worked. "Thanks for giving me a ride." I climbed in and put on my seat belt. "How's Buddy?"

"He's a kleptomaniac."

I laughed. "What does that mean?"

The Accord bumped up and down as Jack made a three- point turn and headed back down my driveway.

"This morning, I found one of Zoe's headbands, my mom's socks, and my grandmother's brush stashed under my bed."

"Interesting collection of items," I said. "If anything goes missing, you know where to check."

"True." The snow started coming down harder as we drove.

"What's the forecast for tonight?" I asked.

"They are guess-timating three or four inches of snow. No ice."

"Do you ever get the feeling the weathermen just throw darts at a board covered with different winter forecasts?"

"It's supposed to be a science," Jack said. "But it doesn't seem very exact."

Betty's was packed, which was good, because I'd rather be busy than bored. Mrs. Banks made an appearance, and I gave her the exact piece of pie she requested. She almost seemed disappointed I didn't argue with her. From my vantage point at the dessert counter, I could see through the windows on the front doors. The snow never let up. Three to four inches was probably a severe understatement.

Jack seemed to be one of the busiest people in the room, ringing out a never-ending line of diners and handling carry-out orders. Through all of it, he smiled and nodded. Was he happier because of Buddy? It was probably nice to go home to a dog that was excited to see you every day. Zoe had told me that after school, Buddy licked Jack's nose, like he was cleaning it. He didn't do that to anyone else, just Jack. It must be some form of exclusive puppy affection.

I knew I couldn't have a pet, because there wouldn't be anyone at home to let it out half the time, and animals needed company. Maybe a cat wouldn't mind having the run of the house when no one was home. Heck, I could probably adopt a cat, and my parents wouldn't notice for a month.

When it was half an hour until the end of my shift, I walked over to Jack. "I need to place a carry-out order because there is a severe lack of groceries at my house."

Chapter Thirteen

JACK

It must suck to never know if there'd be food at home. My grandmother always made sure our house was stocked with enough food to outlast a blizzard and the zombie apocalypse combined.

"Good thing you've got an in with the guy who takes the carry-out orders." I grabbed the order slip and started jotting down items.

"Are you going to wait for me to tell you what I want, or are you making it up as you go along?"

"I know you. You want a burger with everything but onions, and you want sweet potato fries."

She laughed, liked I'd surprised her in a good way. "You do know me."

"I'm going to add the spaghetti family dinner with salad and bread and butter. You can make toast with the bread and butter."

Her smile widened. "Thanks for looking out for me."

Of course I looked out for her. That's what you did for people you cared about. Oh, hell. I did care about her... and not in a sisterly manner. Time to retreat before I said something stupid. "It's the least I can do, since you helped rescue Buddy."

I dropped the order off in the kitchen and then came back to find a line of people waiting to check out. Everyone must have decided the weather had taken a turn for the worse. People around here mostly drove trucks and safe cars rather than sports cars. Driving would be slow, but barring any idiots, we should all make it home just fine.

After the last person checked out, Betty locked the doors and waited for us all to start our cars before she drove off in her Escalade.

Delia held a giant takeout bag on her lap as I drove out of the parking lot. "What all did you order?" she asked.

"It's not all for you. I ordered dinner for myself since they had extra spaghetti."

She inhaled. "It smells awesome."

I drove at a slow pace, because visibility was crap even with my high beams on. I found myself leaning forward and clenching the steering wheel.

"It's getting pretty bad. You can take me to your house instead of making two stops," Delia said.

"I thought about that," I said, "but your place is closer. I might be camping on your couch if this doesn't get any better."

When I pulled down Delia's driveway, I hoped to see some lights on in the house or another car in the driveway.

The house was dark, and the only vehicle in the driveway was her truck. "No one's home?"

"Doesn't look like it." She acted like it was no big deal, but I think it bothered her.

Should I try to make the drive home when I couldn't see a foot in front of the windshield, or should I crash here and keep Delia company?

"Want to come in for a while and wait for the weather to clear up?" she asked.

"Sure. I can eat and then check to see what it's like."

"If it's too bad to drive, the couch is all yours."

We got out of my Accord and trudged up to the front door. I followed Delia inside. Weird that I'd known her forever and had never been in her house before. The table in the foyer was stacked high with mail and newspapers. Were they recycling, or had her parents not had time to go through all the mail? And why were some of the envelopes red? That couldn't be good.

"This way," Delia said.

I followed her into the kitchen and stared. The chrome and aqua appliances looked like they were as old as the farm house, which was cool, but would they even work? Coffee cups were stacked in the sink, and more mail sat on the counter by the toaster.

I set the carry-out bag on the table.

Delia grabbed paper plates from one of the cabinets. "Your grandmother would probably be appalled by our kitchen."

"It's kind of retro cool."

"My parents talked about replacing the appliances, but I love these. Plus we mostly use the Crock-Pot and the coffeemaker, so there really isn't any point."

"Some decorator would probably pay big bucks for these, since they all match." I pulled out Delia's burger and my spaghetti and then put the extra food in the refrigerator, which was empty except for ketchup, mustard, coffee creamer, and string cheese. I almost commented on the lack of food but realized Delia might be self-conscious about it.

I sat at the Formica kitchen table, which had blue stars that matched the appliances, and dug into my container of spaghetti while Delia ate her burger.

"I feel like I need to apologize for my house," Delia blurted out. "Everything at your house always seems so perfect."

"Really?" That was weird. "Our cabinets are stocked, but the house isn't perfect. The steps are warped, and there are cracks in the plaster ceilings upstairs."

"But your grandmother is so organized." She pointed at the counter. "I don't even know what is in those stacks of mail. My dad has a system. Every month, I hope he pays the power on time so the electricity doesn't go out."

"Has that happened before?"

"Yes. And it's not like we didn't have the money to pay the bill. It's just that nothing around here happens on a regular schedule."

"My grandma likes to be prepared for anything." I thought about it. "After she moved back in with us, I think she tried to make up for what my mom didn't do."

"Your mom is a lot better now. Don't you think?"

I rolled spaghetti around my fork. "She is." I wondered how long it would last. If she was back to normal for good. The jaded voice in the back of my head reminded me that if something seemed too good to be true, it probably was.

...

DELIA

Having Jack in my house felt strange. Maybe the reason Zoe and I didn't hang out here more was because I was very aware that my house wasn't up to her family's standards. It's not like it was dirty, but it was kind of cluttered, and we should probably dust more often than we did.

Jack didn't seem to judge me, which was good. Not having to be alone at home was nice. With the way the snow was coming down, camping out here was probably a good plan.

"You should call your mom and let her know where you are."

"I should've thought of that." He pulled out his cell and dialed. I grabbed my own cell and walked into the foyer. Two texts waited for me, asking if I was home. I answered both. My parents said they weren't getting off work until eleven, and they'd check the roads before they tried driving home. I walked back into the kitchen as Jack set his cell on the table. "My mom was on the verge of a freakout when I said I might try driving home, so I told her I'd camp on the couch until it was safe to leave."

"Good plan." I shivered. "I'm going to change into something warmer. Do you want a sweatshirt or something?"

"Sure. And I think I'll make some coffee."

Something warm to drink sounded good. "I'll be back in a minute."

I felt bad that Jack was stuck here but happy I didn't have to ride out the storm alone. Not that I minded quiet time. I did some of my best artwork when I was alone, but it was nice to have someone to talk to.

After changing into yoga pants and a sweatshirt and swapping out the tiara for a headband, I felt warmer and more comfortable. I rooted through my closet and found a one-size-fits-all sweatshirt—which is always a lie—that was way too big for me. It said, "The Earth without art is just Eh."

My dad wouldn't care if I loaned Jack his clothes, so if this didn't work, we'd try something from his closet. The rich scent of coffee drifted upstairs.

In the kitchen, Jack sat at the table finishing off his spaghetti. I held the sweatshirt out to him. "See if this fits."

He examined the art-friendly motto and grinned."That's pretty good." He pulled it over his head, messing up his hair. I had the strange desire to reach out and fix it for him, but that could be awkward.

"If I had the right supplies here, this would be the perfect time to color your hair."

"What a shame," Jack said. "Fate must be looking out for me."

"Who cuts your hair?"

He shrugged. "Whoever has an open chair at Crazy Cuts."

"So you have no plan...you just let them do whatever?"

"As long as it's not in my eyes, I don't care."

"You're so low maintenance," I said. "What's that like?"

"Aren't you the queen of I don't give a crap about what anyone thinks?"

"Most of the time, yes. But no one messes with my hair."

...

DELIA

After we were done eating, I cleaned up the carry-out containers and paper plates. Now what? Television sounded like the most low stress answer. I glanced at him.

Would it be so wrong if I leaned against him on the couch while we watched a movie? The coffeemaker hissed out the last puff of steam, signaling its cycle was done. I grabbed the creamer from the fridge and two cups from the cabinet.

"You take cream and sugar, right?" I said.

"Yes."

Funny that I knew how he liked his coffee. I guess that's what happened when you worked with someone and went to school with them and practically lived at their house.

I carried the coffee into the living room where the love seat was piled high with clean laundry, which meant we'd both have to sit on the couch. Not that I minded. I sat not quite in the middle, giving him about two thirds of the couch real estate. That way he could scoot closer if he wanted to, but it didn't look like I was setting him up.

He took the coffee I held out to him and sat in the middle of the area I'd allotted him. What did that mean? Who knew? It was a bad idea to even think about Jack in a non-brotherly way. I grabbed the remote and hit the guide. There were a couple of movies on I liked, but I didn't think Jack would go for The Princess Bride. Maybe he'd be okay with the Avengers movie.

"If you choose Princess Bride over the Avengers, we are going to have a problem."

"I like both of them, but I can understand why you'd be more into Captain America."

He gave me a look of disbelief. "Iron Man, not Captain America. He's too goody-goody."

Not like I minded watching men run around in superhero costumes, so I clicked on the movie.

The temperature in the room seemed to drop. I set my coffee down and grabbed the afghan off the back of the love seat. Back on the couch, I threw it over my lap and offered part of it to Jack. "You're welcome to share if you're cold."

"I'm good." He kept his eyes on the screen like he was afraid to look at me. What is that about?

Chapter Fourteen

JACK

Why in the hell did it feel like I was on a date? How had I ended up in this position? I should have tried to drive home. Wait. Time to regroup. No need to panic. This was Delia. Not someone I was interested in. But the memory of kissing her in my dream taunted me, making me feel like a liar.

I snuck a glance at her, leaning back on the couch under the afghan she'd offered to share with me. She'd taken off the Pie Princess crown when she'd changed out of her waitress uniform, which had left her hair wild and messy. I no longer thought the hot pink stripes were ridiculous. I thought they were sexy, and that was not right.

It didn't matter if I was cold, sitting next to her on the couch, I would not share an afghan with her out of principle. It would be wrong. The fact that she offered showed she had no ulterior motives. She thought of me like a brother. As she should. I just needed to get my brain back on the right track and not think about how easy it would be to scoot over and share the blanket, move in closer until I could put my arm around her shoulders...lean over until we were lined up just right and then kiss her...at which point, she'd probably freak out and punch me in the nose.

"Why do you have that look on your face?" Delia asked.

"What look?"

"I don't know...you look like you're thinking disturbing thoughts."

Way to be smooth. I shrugged and sunk lower on the couch. "I'm just thinking about the weather and if it would be safe to try and drive home."

"Oh."

Did she sound disappointed? "Unless you want me to stay. I don't have a problem hanging out until your parents come home."

She set her coffee on the end table. "Maybe we should go check on the weather so you'll know if leaving is an option."

Crap. That wasn't what I wanted, but it was probably the smart thing to do. I stood and went to the front door. The window showed swirling white snowflakes. Delia opened the door a few inches, and I moved in close so we could both look outside. It looked like there was a foot of snow on the ground, and more was still falling. "I think I'm camping out." I headed back to the couch. Now that we'd opened the door, I was cold. It couldn't hurt to share an afghan, right?

Back on the couch, I scooted closer."I want joint custody of the afghan."

"Fine. Since you shared your dog, I'll share my afghan."

She shifted the blanket toward me.

I had to sit a few inches from her if we were going to make this work. She kept her eyes on the television screen like my nearness didn't affect her at all. I'd follow her lead and watch the movie. Everything would be fine.

Her cell buzzed. She checked it and frowned, setting the phone down without texting whoever it was back.

"What's wrong?" I asked, knowing it wasn't any of my business.

"Aiden keeps texting me. I don't feel like talking to him."

"So you guys aren't a thing anymore?"

"I'm not sure we ever were a thing. I probably just saw what I wanted to see."

"No. He was into you."

She tilted her head and looked at me. "Why do you say that?"

"He waited for you to get off work. It's a simple fact. A guy doesn't hang around if he's not interested." Damn, had I just confessed that I was interested in her? Would she put two and two together?

"I think he thought he might be interested and then decided I wasn't his type." She shrugged. "As you've told me before, my personality is a lot to take."

Shit. I had said that. "Sorry. That was a jerk thing for me to say."

She looked down at the afghan and picked at a stray thread of yarn. "But it's sort of true, isn't it?"

What was I supposed to say to that? "I think you throw people off-balance sometimes, because you're different. You're not shy, and you don't mind attracting attention."

"Can I tell you a secret?"

I nodded. "Sure."

"I didn't start sewing and changing my clothes around because I wanted to be different. I did it because my mom bought everything at Goodwill, and I didn't want any of the kids at school to see me wearing their cast-offs."

"But both your parents work." Not that there was anything wrong with finding clothes at Goodwill, but having it be the only place you could shop kind of sucked.

"They both owed money for student loans, and my grandmother was in a nursing home for a while. I think they paid for most of her care, so there wasn't much left to go around."

Vulnerability shone in her eyes.

"I don't think anyone would ever guess that's why you created your own stuff. Especially, since you're good at it."

"Thanks. I'm glad my excuse worked. And after a while, it wasn't an excuse any more. I just changed my clothes around because I liked doing it."

"Money is okay now, right?" Or was that why she was working at Betty's?

"Yes, except the water heater and the washing machine both died in the same week. So money is tight now, but nothing like it was when I was a little kid. I wanted to work so I'd have guilt-free money for art supplies."

"That's cool. I understand why you mess around with your clothes, but what's the deal with your hair?"

"It's fun, and it attracts attention. I'd rather stand out than blend in." Her eyes lit up, like she'd just realized something. "What you said earlier about guys not waiting around unless they were interested...did you mean that?"

Damn. Damn. Damn. "Yeah, it's part of the guy code." I turned to face the television because it would be so easy to lean over and kiss her.

...

DELIA

Jack had turned his attention back to the movie. Did he do that to avoid looking at me? He'd given me a ride to work, helped me with my carry-out order, and agreed to come in and have dinner. Sure, the weather was bad, but it wasn't ice- storm bad. Did that mean he liked me, or was he just being a friend?

If I made some sort of move, and he wasn't interested, I'd look like a world-class idiot. Not to mention, I'd been down this road before and vowed never to make the first move again. What if he was interested? It could be awesome. Even though he was a jerk sometimes, he was a good, puppy-rescuing person.

But what about Zoe? How would she deal with it? Would she be mad? Probably at first, but after a while it could be cool...maybe. Then again, why was I worrying about this when Jack thought of me like a sister or, more accurately, a pain in the ass little sister? And it's not like he was mooning over me. He was watching the movie.

"Do you have any popcorn?" he asked.

Wow. Here I was dreaming about kissing him, and he was focused on salty snacks. "I think so. I'll go check."

I headed into the kitchen. What in the hell had I been thinking? It was Jack. Even if he was handsome, had great shoulders and touchable hair, and he smelled good, he was still Jack, the older brother of my best friend. Not a datable guy. He was off-limits.

I made a batch of microwave popcorn and continued to tell myself I'd misunderstood Jack's message. He hadn't been talking about himself after all. He'd been talking about Aiden. Who apparently liked me enough to wait for me and to text me but not to actually date me. While the microwave buzzed in the background, I checked Aiden's text.

He'd been worried about me working tonight and wanted to make sure I was okay. I texted back, All good. I'm home.

He texted back a smile face. So much for a heart to heart conversation. When the timer dinged, I grabbed the bag from the microwave, ripped it open, and poured it in the popcorn pan, adding extra salt.

Jack pointed at the rectangular cake pan I carried back to the couch. "Did you make popcorn or bake a cake?"

I sat and showed him the popcorn in the pan. "This is how we do popcorn."

"Most people use a bowl."

I shrugged. "This is how my mom has always done it."

"Okay." He grabbed a handful of popcorn and shoved it in his mouth.

We watched the movie and ate popcorn and didn't talk. I was oddly aware of how close he was next to me on the couch. I could feel heat radiating off his leg, which was an inch from mine.

When the pan was empty, I set it on the coffee table. My fingers were greasy from the butter, so I grabbed a tissue off the table. I turned to offer Jack a tissue, but he must have leaned over to grab his own because we ended up almost nose to nose.

"Oh." I gave a nervous laugh. "You startled me."

Jack didn't smile. He stared deep into my eyes like I was a puzzle he was trying to figure out. Seconds stretched out as neither of us moved. Would he kiss me? My heart beat loud in my ears as he leaned in a fraction of an inch. Our lips were almost touching. Was he waiting to see if I was okay with this?

He wasn't running away from me, but he wasn't making a move either, so I caved and did it for him. Leaning in, I brushed my lips against his and then held my breath, waiting for his reaction. He stared at me for a moment like he wasn't sure what he wanted to do, and then he kissed me back...gentle at first and then it built into something more. Something a little wild and a whole lot of right. Way more right than kissing Aiden had been. I understood now. This was what kissing was supposed to be like.

I slid my fingers through the hair at the nape of his neck. The kiss became softer, and then it stopped. I opened my eyes, leery of what I might see. He smiled back at me. "I've wanted to do that since you started working at Betty's."

"Really?"

He nodded. "What about you? When did you see me as more than Zoe's brother?"

"In art class," I admitted. "After I drew you."

"Funny how something can be right in front of you and you don't see it." He leaned in and kissed me again, and it was better than the first time, now that I knew he was actually interested in me.

We shifted around, and I must have sat on the remote, because the television volume soared, making me jump. I broke away from Jack as he cracked up laughing.

My face burned. "Where's the stupid remote?"

He found it wedged between the couch cushions and turned the television to normal volume. I sat close to him, where he could put his arm around me, which he did.

And now it seemed awkward. Were we kissing? Were we watching television? Had I ruined the moment? I waited for him to make a move, and this time he did, touching my face so I'd turn toward him. We kissed for I don't know how long before I heard a car door slam.

Jack jumped away from me. "Did you hear that?"

I nodded. "Make sure the television is on something we'd watch. I'll go see who it is."

Hopping up, I ran to the door and saw my mom hiking through foot-deep snow covering the sidewalk. "Hey, Mom, you're home early," I called out.

"Yeah." She made it to the door and hugged me. "They shut the lab down early tonight due to the weather. Whose car is that?"

"Jack drove me home. We were watching a movie." Would she believe me? My cheeks heated, which meant my face was probably turning red. The foyer was kind of dark. Hopefully, she wouldn't notice.

She stomped snow off her boots, hung her coat in the hall closet, and toed off her boots. "Did you bring any carry out home from Betty's?" she asked.

"Spaghetti is in the fridge."

"I knew I raised you right." She headed into the kitchen without another word.

Back in the living room, I found Jack folding the afghan and hanging it on the back of the couch, like he was tidying up and getting ready to leave. He ran his hand back through his hair and stood there looking at me for a moment. "So... your mom's home."

"Yeah...she kind of lives here." I sat on the couch and waited to see what his next move would be.

"I should go." He headed for the front door.

Not the move I expected, but it's not like I was going to argue with him. I'd play along until I figured out what his problem was. I followed him to the foyer. "So...you're leaving?"

"Well...yeah. I mean, your mom's home, so you don't need me to keep you company." He grabbed his coat and shrugged it on, not making eye contact with me. "Besides, Buddy is probably waiting for me."

"Right. You're leaving because of your dog, not because you're freaking out about kissing me."

He looked toward the kitchen, like he was worried my mom might've overheard what I'd said.

"I gotta go."

...

JACK

I took the drive to my house slow, because I needed time to think and because the roads were a little slick. Nothing too scary, but nothing to take for granted, either. What the hell had I been thinking, kissing Delia? There was no way this could end well.

And yeah, I knew she was ticked off at me for bailing on her. Better now than a few weeks from now after we'd spent time together as a couple. Ending this before it started was the smart thing to do. Then again, she could be plotting how to blow up my car.

Wait. This was stupid. Why was I worried about a couple of kisses? In a few days, neither of us would care about this. Right... Kissing her in real life had been way better than kissing her in my dream.

There was no one else on the road at this time of night, which was a good thing because visibility wasn't great. I knew this road so well I could probably drive it in my sleep. Up ahead, I saw a red van pulled off into the field. I slowed down, put my hazards on, and rolled up on the shoulder behind the van. I checked the rearview mirror for oncoming traffic before getting out.

"Hello? Anyone need help?"

No one answered, but I walked to the driver's side and peered in just to make sure. No one was inside, so I climbed back in my car and drove home.

When I walked in the front door, Buddy bounded toward me, his tail a blur.

"Hey, Buddy." I leaned down and picked him up. "Did you miss me?" He licked my nose and barked. Zoe sat up from where she'd been sleeping on the couch. "I'm glad you came home. Buddy wouldn't let me sleep in my bed. He kept whining for me to follow him down here to the door, like I could make you magically appear." She yawned. "It's a good thing he's cute."

"Thanks for taking care of him."

She muttered something, grabbed her pillow, and headed toward the stairs.

"Come on, boy. Let's go to sleep." I carried Buddy up to my room and then lay there, wide awake, staring at the ceiling. Had I made a mistake by blowing Delia off? Who knew? What I needed was a girl who'd make my life simple, predictable, calm. Delia wasn't that girl.

Chapter Fifteen

JACK

I rolled out of bed around nine and headed downstairs to the kitchen with Buddy on my heels.

"I'll share some breakfast with you."

He barked like he thought this was a good plan.

Halfway through my bacon and eggs, Zoe came into the kitchen.

"How did things go at Delia's last night?" she asked.

That was a strange question. Delia wouldn't have told her about us kissing, would she? If she had, I don't think Zoe would be talking to me right now. She'd be ticked. "It was fine. We watched a movie. I stuck around until her mom came home."

"Did she bring out the popcorn pan?" Zoe asked.

I nodded. "Is it just me, or does her family do everything a little bit different?"

Zoe poured herself a glass of milk and joined me at the table. "I've never been able to figure out if her parents do those things because they like to be different or because they never bother to make sure they have the right stuff on hand before they start something."

"It's weird, because even though she has parents, it's like she's on her own. If she hadn't brought carry-out from Betty's, there wouldn't have been any food at her house."

"Sometimes her place reminds me of a haunted house. There's evidence that someone else lives there, but you rarely see them," Zoe said. "I think that's why we spend so much time over here."

"I guess I'll have to stop griping about her hanging around all the time."

"What will you do with all your free time?" Zoe asked.

"Smart-ass. I could go back to griping about Grant."

She grabbed a strip of bacon from my plate. "Nope. You could gripe about Aiden if you want. I don't understand his sudden change of heart."

"Is Delia still interested in him?" Not that I cared.

"I think she's confused about why he only wanted to be friends. It's not like he broke her heart. He just kind of disappointed her," Zoe said. "Is there anyone at work you could fix her up with?"

"Nah." I offered my toast crust to Buddy. He swallowed it without chewing. Rocky would be proud.

"Too bad."

Zoe left, and I sat there grinding my teeth about the thought of Delia with another guy. Then again, it would make my life less complicated if she was off the market.

...

DELIA

After Jack left, I went back into the kitchen for a glass of milk.

"Did I hear Jack leave?" my mom asked.

"Yeah. Since I wasn't home alone anymore, I guess he felt free to bail."

"It was nice of him to stay with you." My mom yawned. "I'm going to sleep." She put her dishes in the sink, hugged me, and then went off to bed.

Soon, I could hear the industrial fan my parents used as a noisemaker going strong upstairs. I went back into the living room and curled up on the couch under the afghan. I could swear a warm, spicy, guy deodorant scent lingered on the couch. I closed my eyes and drifted. What was I going to do about Jack? I may have started the first kiss, but he initiated several after that, so I know he didn't hate kissing me.

Why had he freaked out when my mom came home? Did someone finding out he kissed me make him feel guilty, or was he embarrassed about it? At this point, I wasn't sure if I was merely annoyed or totally ticked off. I needed to talk to someone about this, and my normal go to confidant would be Zoe, but there was no way I could talk to her about her brother. That left only one person who I knew would keep this information a secret, because I'd kept his secret. First thing tomorrow morning, I was calling Aiden. Maybe he could help me figure this out.

Was it even worth it to consider dating Jack? I needed Zoe and her family for a sense of normalcy. No matter what my mom's good intentions were, I knew my life would continue to run on its chaotic course, based on my parents working odd and inconsistent hours. Not that it was their fault. Money didn't grow on trees, and we didn't have any extended family, like Zoe's grandma, to help when times were tough.

My parents were both only children, so I didn't have any cousins or aunts and uncles. In a small town like Canton, where everyone seemed to be related to everyone else, I'd always felt like my family was adrift, paddling on their own, trying to steer a leaking boat in the right direction.

I shifted positions on the couch, trying to get my brain to shut off. It kept spinning out odd scenarios where I kissed Jack and Zoe found out and stopped talking to me. Or I tried to kiss Jack and he told me he wasn't interested. Or I decided to risk it all to date Jack, only to realize he was, in fact, the jerk he'd always been. In none of these scenarios did I end up with any type of happily-ever-after. Maybe my brain was telling me I should focus on finding a different guy. One thing was for sure: I wasn't going to be falling asleep any time soon.

Time to paint. I headed out to my studio and clicked on the overhead lights. During the day, the light coming in through the windows made the place a lot brighter. Now it just looked sad and rundown. One day, I'd turn it into a real studio, but for now, it worked as a place to paint where I didn't have to worry about splattering anything on the floor.

The next morning, I woke to the smell of coffee. Someone must be up. I headed into the kitchen, where my mom sat reading the newspaper.

"Morning, Mom."

"Morning, yourself, sweetie. Today, I'm going to drag your dad to the grocery store, and we're going to stock the house for winter, if you want to come along."

"Maybe. I'm not sure what I'm doing today."

"Any special meal requests?"

I thought about it. "Let's make a list. Otherwise I'll come home to enough mac-n-cheese to last the winter and nothing else."

"You love mac-n-cheese," my mom protested.

I grabbed a piece of paper and a pen. "I do, but it would also be nice to have cereal and stuff for spaghetti, and tuna noodle casserole, and soup and crackers. Stuff that lasts forever but is easy to make."

"We can do that as long as those ingredients are also cheap." She sighed. "We'll probably be playing catch up with the bills for a couple of months, but we should be okay after that."

I'd never really talked finances with my parents. "Both you and dad work a lot of hours. If the washing machine and water heater hadn't both bit the dust at the same time, would we be okay?"

"Your dad and I make decent money. Better than a lot of folks, but we still have to budget our spending." She took the pen and added a few items to the list. "I don't want you to think you ever have to do without. If there is anything you really want, we'll find a way to make it work."

"I'm good."

"How'd things go with Jack last night?" she asked. "Anything romantic in the air?"

"And this conversation is over." I headed upstairs to take a shower, and then I went into my room and called Aiden.

"Hello, Delia. What's up?"

"I need to talk about something confidential, and you're the first person that came to mind."

"Which means it's something you can't tell Zoe," Aiden said. "This should be interesting."

"Did I mention that you aren't allowed to judge me?"

He laughed. "I'd never do that and, of course, I'll keep whatever it is secret, so go ahead."

Why did it feel like I was confessing to some sordid affair? "I kissed Jack."

"What?"

Aiden's voice came through so loud I had to move my cell away from my ear.

"That was a little loud and kind of judge-y."

"Sorry. You just surprised me. Not that I want gory details, but how did this happen?"

I told him the story about Jack giving me a ride and how he'd been so nice about the food, and then I threw in how we'd rescued Buddy together, just to give him a little context. "So he used to be a jerk, but then he saved a puppy, and he knows how you like your hamburgers so you kissed him."

"When you say it like that, it sounds stupid." I paced back and forth in my room. "And you're supposed to be helping me figure this out, not making me feel like an idiot."

"Fine. How did you leave things with him?"

"That's the worst part." I shared how Jack had bolted. "And now I don't know if I'm supposed to act like we've never kissed or what."

"To figure this out, I need to ask you some questions."

"Okay." This was what I needed, another person's perspective.

"Do you like him, or was he convenient?"

At first his question ticked me off, but he made an interesting point. "I think I really like him."

"Because he saves puppies?"

"That's part of it."

"Do you think he regretted kissing you, or do you think he bailed because he didn't know how to deal with the fact that he wanted to kiss you?"

"Is there some new mind-reading app I'm unaware of? How am I supposed to know what he was thinking?"

"As a guy, I'm guessing he left because he didn't want to deal with feelings."

"Whose feelings...his or mine?"

"Both, probably. What you need to do is see if he's really interested or not. Maybe go out with someone else and see if he gets jealous."

It's not like guys were lining up to sweep me off my feet. "Am I supposed to make a date magically appear?"

"No. You and I could pretend to date, which might help with a problem I've been having. My dad has been asking me why I don't bring any girls around, which makes me wonder if he suspects the truth. Not that I'm ashamed of who I am, but I'm not ready to go to war with him just yet."

"How would us pretending to date help my situation?"

"Word will get back to Jack, and then he'll have to decide if he wants to make a move, and then you'll know if he's worth stressing over."

"Okay. So if he's really interested, he'll come back around like some sort of Boyfriend Boomerang?"

"Exactly," he said. "That sounds like a Sherlock Holmes case. Operation Boomerang Boyfriend is afoot."

"Do you want me to make you a Sherlock Holmes hat?" I teased.

"No, but if you could get Benedict Cumberbatch to talk to me, I'd be okay with that."

And suddenly I knew what our first fake date would be. "How would you feel about binge-watching Sherlock on Netflix?"

"We could do that, but first we should be seen together in public so Jack hears about it."

It was almost like my life had turned into some sort of twisted reality television show where the guy I had wanted to date was asking me on a date to convince the new guy I might want to date that I was worth dating.

"Before we start Operation Boomerang Boyfriend, I think I should give Jack a chance to figure things out." The last thing I wanted to do was push him away.

"You're probably right, but I don't have any plans tonight, do you?"

"Nope."

"Want to hang out with Zoe and Grant at Edison's?" he asked. "It doesn't have to be part of some master Sherlock-type plan. We can go as friends."

"Sounds good."

...

JACK

Trevor sat in the recliner in his living room, gloating like he'd been right all along.

"I didn't tell you I kissed Delia so you could be an ass." I sat on the couch, scratching Rocky's ears.

"Technically, she kissed you," Trevor pointed out. "Which is way better because you know she likes you. Of course, then you had to go and screw it up."

"I didn't screw it up. I strategically retreated. There's a difference."

"Really? How big of a window do you think you have where she'll forgive you for bailing?"

Good question. "Maybe it's better if she doesn't. I mean, it is Delia. She's capable of some scary things."

"Is there another girl you're interested in?" he asked.

"There are some cute girls at school. I could ask one of them out if I wanted to."

"And yet you're at my house on a Saturday night, and we're both dateless."

"By choice," I said. "I could've asked Delia out, and you could ask out any girl you want." Rocky shifted around and made a grumbling sound. "As long as she liked dogs."

"Why would I want to be around anyone who didn't like dogs?" Trevor stood. "Let's get out of here."

"Where to?"

"How about Edison's?"

Zoe was going out with Grant tonight. What would Delia be doing? Probably going to that weird Art of Tea place, so the odds of bumping into her at Edison's were slim. "Works for me."

We had to circle Edison's parking lot twice before I found a place to park. "This is not a good sign."

"It's probably a bunch of little kid parties," Trevor said. "And they don't play air hockey, so we should be okay."

Inside the arcade, a sea of elementary kids ran amuck. There was a group of little girls wearing Disney princess dresses, a group of boys waving fake foam pirate swords, and a mixed group of boys and girls wearing neon yellow shirts emblazoned with the words "Happy Birthday, Lilly and Leo."

"I'm guessing Lilly and Leo's parents don't want to lose any kids," Trevor said.

"I guess not." I pointed toward the air hockey tables. "Let's start over there."

Half an hour later, we'd each won two games. "This is the tie breaker," I said.

"Hey, is that Delia?" Trevor asked.

I didn't fall for it. "Sorry, you'll have to do better than that to distract me."

"No." Trevor picked up his striker. "Timeout. For real. I think she's over there with your sister."

"Seriously?" I turned to see what he was talking about. Sure enough, Delia and Zoe were walking over to the restaurant side. They weren't alone. Grant and Aiden followed behind them.

"I thought you said she wasn't dating that guy anymore," Trevor said.

"She said she wasn't."

"Was that before or after your disappearing act?"

Well, hell. "He friend-zoned her, so this doesn't make any sense."

"Unless they're here as friends," Trevor said.

"Maybe." Not like I cared. If she wanted to be with Aiden, it was none of my business. Heck, it might make my life easier if she was back together with him. Then I wouldn't be the bad guy. She'd just be the girl who moved on.

"Earth to Jack," Trevor said. "Are you ready to lose?"

Right. This game decided the winner of our air hockey tournament. I turned back around and concentrated on smacking the flat puck across the table into Trevor's goal. I must have been preoccupied with something, because he stopped all of my shots and won in a few moments.

"That was just sad." Trevor set his striker down. "Want to get some pizza so you can eavesdrop on Delia and her date to see how badly you screwed up?"

"I am hungry." Which was true. So I wasn't going over there to spy on Delia. It was just an interesting coincidence.

Of course, Zoe saw us coming. She waved. I waved back but kept walking, keeping my distance so I wouldn't have to deal with Delia or her date.

The plan might have worked if Delia hadn't stared straight at me with the intensity of the sun like she was waiting for me to make a move. I caved and did the smile and nod maneuver reserved for friends. She nodded back and then turned away from me.

There. See. It wasn't a big deal. Right. If that was true, then why did it feel like someone was playing air hockey in my stomach?

"Smooth," Trevor commented as we sat at the table farthest away from Delia.

"Shut up." I hadn't done that bad.

Chapter Sixteen

DELIA

I leaned over to Aiden. "Should I go over there and ask Jack to join us, just to mess with him?"

"No. Give him time to think about what he wants. Right now, he's probably in denial. A subject I am quite familiar with." He grinned. "He's probably trying to figure out if we're here on a date or as friends."

After we finished eating, Zoe said, "Time for a bathroom break."

I stood to follow her.

Aiden said, "You're going because she's going?"

"Yep. I'm a girl. That's how it works." I followed Zoe to the restroom and checked my makeup in the mirror. Some of my winged eyeliner had migrated, so I dabbed at it with a wet paper towel.

"What's going on with you and Aiden?" Zoe asked.

"When Grant picked me up, he said we were meeting you guys here. Why did I have to hear it from him?"

I'd been afraid she'd ask a bunch of questions. "Aiden called me and asked if I wanted to hang out as friends. We talked for a while, and I decided it couldn't hurt. It's not like I had any other plans tonight, since you were going out with Grant. I didn't think you'd mind."

"Of course, I don't mind you joining us, but I do mind not being the first one to know about it."

"Sorry, it came up all of a sudden, and I just jumped in with both feet."

"Did Jack have anything to do with you being ready to be friends again?" Zoe asked.

I froze for a second. "Why would he?"

"He asked what the deal was with you and Aiden. I thought maybe you guys talked about it last night."

"Nope. We mostly watched movies and ate popcorn." And shared some lip gloss-melting kisses, but that was not something I could talk to her about.

"So you're okay with being friends?" she asked.

"With Jack?"

"What?" She laughed. "No. With Aiden."

Time to cover up my mistake. "I'm good with being Aiden's friend."

"Why did you say that about Jack?"

Crap. Crap. Crappity crap. "It's been us against him for so long, but now he seems like a nice guy. I wasn't sure you were okay with me being friends with him."

She pulled a tube of lip gloss from her pocket. "Maybe the separate car thing really did do the trick, because he isn't as mean as he used to be."

The rest of my non-date was a no pressure event where I had fun with Aiden and Jack moped in the background. Huh. Maybe seeing me with someone else would spur Jack into action.

After an hour of playing some games, it was time to go. Zoe grinned at me like she was the happiest person in the world as she headed off with Grant to his shiny little black sports car in the parking lot. As I walked toward Aiden's beige Volvo, I wondered how happy she'd be for me if she knew I'd kissed Jack.

"It's kind of funny that we might have tricked Jack, even though we weren't trying to trick him." Aiden started the car and shifted into drive once I'd fastened my seat belt. With his hands placed exactly on ten and two on the steering wheel, he drove us out of the parking lot.

"I wish I knew what Jack thought when he saw us together."

"He checked our table several times, which means he was thinking about you," Aiden said. "So that's a good sign."

"I guess." My life would be so much easier if I liked someone who wasn't my best friend's brother. Or if he didn't like me. And who knows? Maybe he didn't. Maybe that was why he'd bolted from my house. "Do you think I should just walk away and look for someone else?"

"If there's no one else you're interested in, why not give him some time and see how it all turns out? If you run across another guy you're interested in, stop worrying about Jack and focus on him."

He'd just hit on part of my problem with this whole situation. "Maybe I shouldn't have kissed Jack, just like I shouldn't have kissed you."

"I don't know. As a guy, it's nice when the other person makes the first move, because it's not so much of a risk. Maybe Jack isn't a risk taker. Tell me more about him."

"Jack never seemed too complex. Before this happened, I would have thought he'd be the one to kiss the girl he liked."

"You've pointed out that my beige Volvo matches my personality: practical, kind of shy like I want to blend into the crowd. Jack drives that old Honda Accord which has seen better days. And Zoe said they offered to let him trade it in, but he refused. Maybe he doesn't like change or is afraid to take a chance on something new."

His argument didn't hold water. "But I'm not something new. He's known me forever."

Aiden slowed down to take the left turn onto the highway. "He's known you all his life, but now he's seeing you as someone else. Maybe he needs a little time to adjust."

I tapped my foot on the floorboard. "Why does it sound like you're defending him?"

"I'm not. I'm figuring out possible explanations for his behavior. You know I like to understand everything. This is me trying to figure out Jack for you. Would you rather I say he's a jerk and you're better off without him?"

"No. I want you to be honest. Why is dating so complicated? My mom and dad met when they were juniors in high school, and they've been inseparable ever since. I thought that's how life worked. You find your person, and everything falls into place."

"My dad was married once before," Aiden said. "It only lasted a few years. Then he met my mother, they were married, and I came along about a year later."

"Is it weird knowing he was married to someone else? How did they tell you?"

"When my grandmother passed away, I helped my mom go through her things. There was a wedding album of my dad with another woman. I showed it to my mom, and she told me he'd been married and divorced before they even met. Like it was no big deal. And I guess it's not, but it still feels weird that he had some other life."

...

JACK

"Do you think they were on a date?" I asked Trevor as we drove home from Edison's.

"I don't know."

It's not like she kissed Aiden. At least not where I could see it. "He never put his arm around her shoulders."

"True," Trevor said. "If they had been on a date, would you care?"

"I don't know."

"You're the only one who knows what you want," Trevor said. "You better figure it out quick, because Christmas is coming up in two weeks."

He'd lost me. "What does that have to do with Delia?"

"It's a universal law. All girls want to have a boyfriend for Christmas."

"Where does that logic come from?" I asked.

"'All I Want for Christmas is You.' 'I'll Have a Blue Christmas Without You.' 'Santa Bring My Baby Back to Me.'"

"Are you just throwing out Christmas song titles like that's supposed to make some sort of sense?" I didn't get it.

"Hello. They're all about having a boyfriend for Christmas. Girls love those songs. Trust me, Delia wants a boyfriend for Christmas, and she might date Aiden just to have someone around."

That would suck. "She's not a girly-girl like that."

"Really? You kissed her, ran away, and then she showed up where you were with another guy. You don't think she planned that?"

"What? No. I mean, how could she? I didn't even know we were going to Edison's until after we made plans at your house."

"I guess you're right. There aren't a ton of things to do around here," Trevor said.

After I dropped him off, I drove home past Delia's house. It's not like it was out of the way. Okay. Yes, it was. I just wanted to see if Aiden's stupid beige Volvo was parked in her driveway. What type of guy drove a beige car? That color should be reserved for great-grandmas. Beige? It was almost a non-color.

His ugly car wasn't taking up real estate in front of Delia's house. Thank goodness. My shoulders relaxed, and I stopped squeezing the crap out of the steering wheel for the rest of the drive home.

When I made it into the house, Buddy bounded over to me. I picked him up and laughed as he washed my face with his tongue. It was gross, but you could tell it meant he loved me, so I let him do it. "Who's a good boy?"

Ruff!

"That's right. You are. Are you hungry?" He wiggled so hard I had to set him down. He ran into the kitchen to his bowl, which I filled with kibble my grandmother had picked up at the vet when she'd taken him for his check-up. Thankfully, he'd gotten a clean bill of health.

After Buddy finished his food and I polished off a bowl of cereal, I went to bed with Delia on my brain. What did I want from her? I wasn't sure, and I hated that there seemed to be a time limit creeping up on me. As if the holidays weren't stressful enough around my house. Then again, Thanksgiving hadn't been that bad. Maybe Christmas didn't have to be awful.

The next morning, I woke up totally disoriented. What in the hell had I been dreaming about? I closed my eyes and tried to remember the oddly vivid dreams.

I'd been driving home from work when my car died. Delia had driven by in her truck with Zoe. She'd looked right at me, and I'd expected her to stop and give me a ride, but she hadn't even slowed down, just blasted by me, and I'd choked on the dust stirred up in her wake.

Once the air cleared, I continued walking, but the ground turned into a swamp intent on sucking me under. I managed to crawl from the muck only to fall down a hill into some kind of cavern. The only light in the cave came from what I thought were glowing stones lining the walls. Then the stones blinked, and I realized they weren't stones; they were eyes. Dozens of creatures were watching me, and I had the feeling if I tried to run, they'd pounce and I'd never get out alive.

What in the hell did that dream mean? I rubbed the sleep out of my eyes. Was my brain trying to warn me that Delia might reject me or that everyone would be watching us? And what did the swamp have to do with anything? Who knew?

Thankfully, it was Sunday, and I wasn't scheduled to work. The only question was would Delia be invading the house? I listened, waiting to hear any conversation that might drift up through the heating vents from the kitchen. All was quiet, which was weird. I grabbed my cell off the nightstand and squinted against the retinal blast it gave off. Was that an eight or a three? My eyes adjusted to the light. It was a three. Why was I awake at three in the morning? Stupid dream.

I rolled over and slammed my eyelids shut, willing my brain to calm down. Seriously...why was I worrying about Delia? Like Trevor pointed out, she kissed me, so she had to like me. That didn't mean she didn't like Aiden, too, and she'd wanted him before she even thought about dating me. Not a comforting thought and I needed to figure out what I wanted.

Maybe I should focus on something else. Christmas was two weeks away. Buddy snored from the bottom of my bed. He was pretty much all I wanted for Christmas. I reached down and scooped him up so I could lay him down beside me. He gave a sleepy yawn, cuddled against me, and went back to snoring.

Did I really want the pain of having a girlfriend, paying attention to her moods, trying to figure out what she wanted?

Maybe I should just stick with my dog.

I woke up a second time to laughter drifting up through the vents. It only took me thirty seconds to realize one of the voices belonged to Delia. Should I go down in my pajamas or change into real clothes? She liked to give me crap about my bedhead, so I'd go down to the kitchen just like I was and see how she reacted.

After brushing my teeth, I picked up Buddy and carried him down the stairs. Delia and Zoe sat at the kitchen table eating pancakes.

"I was wondering when the smell would wake you," my grandmother said from her spot at the stove where she poured fresh batter into a pan. "Do you want pecan or blueberry?"

"Both," I said.

"Great minds think alike," Delia said.

I glanced at her plate of blueberry pecan pancakes and then up at her face. She smiled at me, and my heart rate kicked up a notch, so I smiled back. "Morning."

"Good morning." She pointed at my shirt, which had Captain America's shield on the front. "I thought you were team Iron Man."

I took the plate of pancakes my grandmother held out to me and joined her and Zoe at the table. "They were out of Iron Man in my size. Plus, I like the design of the shield."

"Someone might be getting Iron Man pajamas for Christmas," she said.

"Nah, Santa will probably just bring me dog toys." I dug into my pancakes, amazed at how not awkward it felt being around Delia.

"I've seen dog coats that look like super hero capes," Zoe said. "Buddy might need one of those." Her cell buzzed. She checked the text. "Looks like I need to call Grant to rescue him from the stack of interior decorating magazines his mom is trying to show him." She stood and left the kitchen, dialing her phone as she went.

I wanted to say something to Delia about what had happened between us, but I didn't know what to say. Sorry I panicked and bailed? That didn't sound right. Maybe I'd just ask straight out what I wanted to know. "Did you have fun with Aiden last night?"

"We always have fun together." She poured more syrup on her pancakes. "And it's not like anyone else asked me on a date."

Well, shit. "So you guys are like together now?"

"I never said that." She tilted her head and stared at me like she was issuing a challenge. "I said no one else asked me on a date."

Wait a minute. Did that mean she wanted me to ask her on a date?

"Don't strain your brain trying to figure the situation out," Delia said.

Chapter Seventeen

DELIA

Jack looked like he was trying to solve a complicated equation. Should I take pity on him? He'd walked away from me without explanation, so why should I make this any easier on him?

He glanced over at his grandmother, who was making another round of pancakes like he was worried she might be listening to our conversation. "I don't understand."

"That is becoming quite apparent." I took another bite of the world's best pancakes.

Jack shoveled in his breakfast and then sighed. "I should take Buddy out for a walk. Do you want to go with us?"

Was that his way of trying to get me alone so we could talk? "Sure."

I grabbed my coat from the hook by the front door and watched as Jack tried to attach a camouflage leash to Buddy's collar. Buddy was doing some wiggle butt pounce and play dance of happiness, making it difficult for Jack to accomplish the task.

"Want some help?" I asked.

"See if you can pick him up," Jack said.

"I have a better idea." I sat down on the floor and patted my lap. "Come here, puppy."

Buddy galloped over and climbed onto my legs. He looked up at me and then licked my chin. "He's so cute it almost hurts."

"I know." Jack managed to click the leash onto Buddy's collar. He wiggled off my lap and bounded for the door.

I stood and followed them out. "Does he really need a leash?"

"I know we don't have to worry about a lot of traffic out here, but I don't want him taking off after a rabbit and getting lost. He's still a baby, and he isn't trained yet, so it's not worth the risk."

Buddy romped in a zig-zag pattern from bushes to leaves to specific blades of grass that he thought he needed to pee on as we walked around the side of the house. "I see your point. He doesn't exactly have a plan, does he?"

"Do you?" Jack asked.

It felt like I'd missed a beat in the conversation. "Do I what?"

He stopped walking and turned to face me so we were toe to toe. His big brown eyes rivaled Buddy's as he spoke. "Do you have a plan about us?"

With him being so close, I had trouble forming coherent sentences. "I...no...not a plan...more like a hope."

The corners of his mouth quirked up in an I'm sexy even though I have bedhead and I'm wearing a Captain America T shirt covered in dog fur kind of grin. "And what are you hoping for?"

That he would shut up and kiss me but I couldn't exactly blurt that out. And I would not tell him that I wanted him to ask me on a date. I took the leap of faith last time, so it was his turn. "Well, I was hoping we could see if there is an us."

He leaned in closer. "It will be complicated," he said, "with Zoe."

As if I hadn't realized that. "I know." My lips tingled in anticipation as he tilted his head to the right and leaned down to press his lips against mine.

Ruff, ruff, ruff, ruff!

I jerked away from Jack to look at Buddy. Jack mirrored the move, which left both of us glancing around trying to figure out what Buddy had barked at.

"Not cool, Buddy." Jack laughed awkwardly. "I expected there to be a lion charging us."

"A lion...in southern Illinois."

"That wasn't a oh look at the pretty flowers kind of bark. It was a you are in grave danger from a wild animal kind of bark."

Buddy sat and tilted his head, looking up at us like he didn't have a care in the world. The romantic mood had completely evaporated. "So I guess this is one of those to be continued later kind of moments," I said.

"When?" Jack asked. "You're here to see my sister today, so it's not like we can sneak off together."

We could, but I wanted a real date, not a secret rendezvous. "Zoe is meeting Grant for lunch, so I'll be leaving soon. You could come to my house, and we could go grab lunch somewhere."

"I'm going over to Trevor's later. You could come with me."

I was surprised by the offer. I wasn't sure I was ready to hang out in public before we knew what we were doing.

"Or not." He quickened his pace and headed toward the front of the house.

Crap. "Wait." I hustled to catch up with him, but he kept moving. By the time I made it into the house, he was halfway up the stairs to his room, and I couldn't exactly follow him.

"Hey," Zoe called out from the kitchen, "I'm in here."

As if I'd be interested in talking to anyone else in the house. I needed to cover why I'd been outside, in case it looked suspicious. "Buddy is seriously adorable."

"I know." Zoe grinned. "I kind of like it when Jack leaves, because I can have Buddy all to myself."

My cell rang. It was Aiden. "Hello?"

"Delia, do you usually have plans on Thursday nights?"

"That's a random question. What's up?"

"My father is receiving an award in a few weeks, and there's going to be a small dinner to celebrate. I was hoping you'd go with me as my fake date."

I glared at the stairs where Mr. Moody had disappeared. "Sure."

"Cool. Thank you. It's on a Thursday. I'll fill you in on the details when I get them."

I ended the call and set my cell on the counter. "What was that about?" Zoe asked.

"Aiden's dad is getting an award for something, and he asked me to go with him."

"Like a date?" Zoe said. "Because that sounds like a date."

How could I explain without actually explaining? "I think it's more of a friend thing. He just needs someone to go with him so his dad won't give him crap about being antisocial."

"Are you sure he's not trying to suck you back in?" Zoe asked.

"Nope. We've had the talk. He knows where he stands."

Zoe looked at the clock. "Not to kick you out, but I need to get in the shower."

"Got it. Have fun with Grant."

Zoe ran up the stairs as Jack came down them, freshly showered.

He walked past me, grabbing my hand, and tugging me along with him into the laundry room.

"Hello to you, too."

"Why don't you want to go to Trevor's?"

"I never said I didn't want to go. I just wanted to ask a question, and you ran away from me, again."

He ducked his head. "Fine. Ask."

"Who will be there, and how will we act? Can we act like a couple in front of other people, or should we tell Zoe first?"

"How about we don't act and we just do whatever seems right?"

That left so much open to interpretation, but I was willing to give it a shot. "Okay."

"Good. I'll follow you to your house. You can drop off your truck, and we'll go to Trevor's."

...

JACK

After Delia left, I called Trevor and explained the situation. "Glad to see you're making a move," Trevor said.

"And you'll be cool about it," I said.

"Of course...most of the time. I might have to bring up some embarrassing moments just so she knows what she's getting into."

"Don't even think about it." I hung up and headed out the door.

For once, Delia's truck wasn't the only vehicle in her driveway. I considered honking for her to come out, but that was more of a friend thing than a date thing. If we really were going to date, I should do it right.

I parked and climbed out of my car. Before I made it to the front door, Delia came around from the side of the house.

"What were you doing outside?" I asked.

"It's weird the things you don't know about." She turned back the way she'd come from. "Follow me."

She led me to the side door of a garage that had seen better days. The entire structure leaned to the right. "Are you sure this is safe?"

"I wouldn't suggest punching a wall, but other than that, it's fine." She opened the door and went inside. I followed into what must be her art studio.

There were several easels set up with works in progress. An old sink was on a wall next to a shelf holding mason jars full of paintbrushes and palette knives. A rickety wooden bench was pushed to one side.

"Is this your secret clubhouse?" I asked.

"More like my secret art studio." She seemed to be waiting for my reaction. "It's cool."

"It's not, but it's functional. One day I plan to decorate it and make it nice and homey, but for now, I spend my money on art supplies."

"I called Trevor and told him you were coming with me. He'll probably try to embarrass me."

"That must be some sort of male bonding ritual," she said. "It won't work because I've known you forever, so there aren't a lot of deep dark secrets he can reveal."

"I'm sure he'll come up with something. Let's go."

When I pulled up to Trevor's, there were a dozen cars in the driveway.

"Are there normally this many people here?" Delia asked.

"It depends. Sometimes his cousins come over on Sundays, and sometimes not. They're in college or older, but they're pretty cool. His whole family is pretty laid back."

"I'm used to that," said Delia.

I didn't think of her family as laid back, I thought of them as absent, but I'd never say that out loud. "Let's do this."

We headed to the fire pit out back. Rocky met us halfway. He bounded up to me. "Hey, boy. This is Delia. She's dog- people, too." I rubbed Rocky's ears while he gave Delia the side-eye. She came closer and held her hand out so he could sniff it.

"What do you say, Rocky? Do I pass inspection?" She scratched under his chin. He leaned into the scratching and sighed.

"I think he likes you." Trevor came walking toward us with a grin on his face, which I knew spelled trouble for me.

"I didn't know you were a dog person," Trevor said to Delia.

"Neither did I, but after hanging around Buddy, I can see a dog in my future."

"Why not now?" Trevor asked.

"My parents work weird hours, so no one would be home to take care of him. And that wouldn't be fair to the dog."

"Yeah, dogs need people," Trevor said. "Speaking of people, do you want me to introduce you to my entire family or just chat with people as they come over to say hello?"

"Let's go with plan B," Delia said. "Sounds less awkward."

"Oh, it will be awkward either way," Trevor said. "Because Jack has never brought anyone with him before."

"Really?" Delia turned to me.

I was going to punch Trevor in the face for this later. "No big deal." Maybe I should have thought this through before I invited Delia to join me. "Who wants a drink?" I headed for the coolers on the patio where they kept the soda. I grabbed a Coke for myself and one for Delia.

She took the can and smiled. "Thanks."

"So what's the deal with you two?" Trevor asked.

Delia pointed at Trevor. "Knock it off. We're still trying to figure this out, and you giving him crap isn't going to help the situation."

"Fine." Trevor laughed. "Let's go sit by the fire pit."

Delia sat next to me, close enough so I could put my arm around her shoulders if I scooted over a little bit. I still wasn't sure where this was going and how much we wanted to let people in on the situation. Who knew if it would last?

Rocky came over and sat on my foot, leaning against my leg. I reached down to rub his head. "Has Rocky done anything interesting lately?"

"He may or may not have eaten a carrot cake my mom left out on the counter to defrost."

"And you know this because..." Delia asked.

"We found the chewed-up box in my mom's closet."

"That darn cat framed you again, didn't he, Rocky?" I scratched under his collar, and he made a happy growling noise.

"Cats don't eat cake," Trevor said.

"I didn't know dogs ate cake," Delia said.

"Rocky eats anything he can grab," Trevor said. "I read online that dogs are opportunists. If they can reach something, they consider it fair game. They're not being bad; they're just taking what the universe is offering them."

"That's very optimistic of them," Delia said, "and it kind of makes sense."

Chapter Eighteen

DELIA

Maybe that's what Jack and I were doing...taking advantage of a situation when the universe offered it. I sat back and sipped my soda while I watched Jack and Trevor talk. Rocky came over and laid his head on my lap.

"Hey, there." I scratched under his chin. He leaned in closer so I'd hit the spot he wanted, and then he half fell onto my lap. I set my drink down, laughing. "You're a little big for a lap dog."

"I don't think he realizes how big he is," Trevor said.

"Do you think Buddy will grow up to be a large lap dog?" I asked Jack.

"The vet said he'd be medium sized...whatever that means."

My cell buzzed, causing Rocky to relocate. "Sorry, pup." I pulled out my cell and frowned. It was Aiden. Now wasn't the time to talk with him, so I set the phone down.

"Who was that?" Jack asked.

I considered lying to him, but I didn't. "Aiden."

"The guy you aren't dating?" Trevor said.

"Yes," I said. "The guy I sometimes hang out with as a friend."

"Because he friend-zoned you," Jack said.

"Yes, and unless you want to be idiot-zoned, I suggest you change the topic."

Trevor stood. "I suddenly feel the need to check on when the food will be ready." And he dashed away.

"Idiot-zoned?" Jack didn't seem to see the humor in my statement.

"Not to be rude, but when I tell you Aiden and I are friends, it's because that's how we work best. I didn't see it at first, but now I do. So I'm friends with him. That's it."

"Maybe I just don't like it because you liked him first, and the only reason you're not with him now is because he didn't want to be with you...not because you didn't want him."

If a guy said something like that to Zoe, she would have gone all drama-queen on him. While I wasn't prone to her overly emotional responses, I was starting to get ticked off.

"Let me make this easy for you. Earlier today, I hoped you'd kiss me, but Buddy kind of interfered. Right now, I'm here with you. Aiden called, and I ignored him in favor of being with you, even though you're being slightly pissy about the whole situation." I probably shouldn't have said that last part, and it would be so much easier if I could just tell him Aiden was gay, but that wasn't my secret to share.

"So you don't want to kiss him?" Jack asked.

"Nope." I waited to see how he'd deal with this information.

"Food's ready," Trevor called out. "Come grab a plate."

"I think we just hit another one of those to be continued later moments." Jack stood. "Let's go get some food."

"Okay." Funny how Jack chose to walk away from an issue rather than hashing it out. Now that I thought about it, that seemed to be his standard operating procedure. When things became complicated, he bailed. Maybe I was being too hard on him. This wasn't the time or place to have a deep discussion.

We sat and ate with Trevor and his family. It was nice. I could see why Jack liked to spend time over here. It filled in the missing piece of having guys to hang around with, but there was more to it than that. I knew Trevor's older brother had OD'd. Everyone knew the story. Yet here these people were, living their lives, moving forward, making the best of what they had left. It was inspiring.

On the drive back to my house, I said, "Trevor and his family seem really great."

"They are."

"I understand why you like to hang out over there every weekend. Thanks for taking me with you."

A comfortable silence settled between us. When Jack pulled up to my house, my dad's truck was gone, and the house was dark.

"No one's home again?" Jack said.

"They probably ran to the store or something," I said.

"Do you guys ever have family time?" Jack asked.

"You mean where my mom cooks and we all sit around the table and talk like normal people?" I frowned. "That happens about twice a month. Usually on Sundays. My mom didn't mention anything about dinner tonight, so I don't know what's happening."

"And that sucks," Jack said.

"Yeah, sometimes it does." It was nice that he understood. "Want to come in for a few minutes while I figure out what's going on?"

"Sure."

When I opened the front door, silence greeted me. I hung up my coat and went into the kitchen. "My mom usually leaves a note to let me know where they are."

On the kitchen table, I spotted a note scribbled on the back of an envelope: Shopping. Back by six with food. See you then.

The clock on the kitchen wall said four p.m., so they wouldn't be gone too long. Maybe Jack and I could get back to our to be continued later scenario. I started to say something, but Jack grabbed my hand and pulled me toward the living room. The couch was covered in clean laundry, but the love seat was clear.

"I guess we're sitting here." Jack sat.

"Have we reached the to be continued later portion of the day?" I asked.

"Yes. I think there were two of those. So I can kiss you, or you can tell me how you aren't interested in Aiden." He sat and put his arm up on the back of the couch like he was just chilling out. "You choose."

I crossed my arms over my chest. "Shouldn't me kissing you prove I'm not interested in someone else?"

"Probably." He patted the couch cushion beside him. "Sit. Reassure me."

I plopped down next to him. "Promise you won't run away like you did last time?"

"Not my best moment," he conceded. "This happening between you and me is kind of big."

"I know. That's why we need to make sure it's worth the potential drama."

He leaned over and pressed his mouth against mine, and everything seemed to fall into place. His arms went around my shoulders as he pulled me closer. The rest of the world faded away. It didn't matter whose brother he was or whose friend I was. We fit together just right.

Jack's cell buzzed. For about five seconds, he froze while he seemed to be figuring out if he should answer his phone. And then he continued kissing me. I ranked higher than his cell. Good to know.

My cell buzzed, which was weird since Zoe was out on a date and my parents were at the store. I ignored whoever it was and focused on Jack. When his cell buzzed again, I pulled away from him. "Is the universe messing with us or something?"

"I don't know. Let's see what's going on." He grabbed his phone and frowned. "Both of mine were from Zoe. She wants me to call her."

I checked my text, and a chill ran down my spine. "Crap. Mine was, too." I dialed and waited while the phone rang and rang.

"I'll try texting her," Jack said.

Neither of us had any luck. "Call your mom. I'll keep trying Zoe."

Jack stood and paced while he listened to his phone.

What the heck was going on? Everything from Zoe being in a car crash to his grandma having a heart attack scrolled through my brain.

I texted Zoe again and waited, trying to keep my freakout under wraps because Jack needed my support. He didn't need me to add to his stress.

Minutes ticked by, adding to the tension. "Maybe we should just go to your house," I said, "since no one is answering."

Jack stopped pacing. "Can you...would you call the hospital...and make sure my family—"

"Got it." I pulled up the number for the local hospital on my cell and dialed. When I asked the emergency room nurse if anyone with the last name of Cain had been admitted, she said, "No." I asked a few more questions before hanging up. "No one named Cain has been admitted for anything. There haven't been any accidents or heart attacks or anything involving anyone who matches the description of Zoe, your grandmother, or your mom."

Jack sat on the couch and closed his eyes. "Thank you. I know it's stupid, but—"

"It's not stupid." I sat and held his hand, lacing my fingers between his. "You've endured enough family trauma to last a lifetime."

My cell buzzed. I checked it. "Holy crap. Zoe wanted to ask my opinion about a Christmas gift for Grant." I texted her back that the sweater she'd taken a picture of at the mall when Grant hadn't been looking was a little too old-man for my taste. Then I added, You just took ten years off your brother's life.

Zoe texted back. Why are you with my brother?

"I think we've just been made," I told Jack, showing him the texts.

"Shit. Tell her you left your phone at our house and I just stopped by to drop it off."

"I'd rather tell her we were hanging out together, or maybe we should just tell her the truth." As far as I was concerned, we were a good fit. And we had spent the afternoon together at Trevor's, which meant we'd been seen together in public already. Not that I was ready to say we were flying off to Vegas for the weekend, but I think it would be okay to say we were dating.

"That's not a good idea."

"I don't want to lie to her." It just didn't feel right.

"It may be stupid, but I'm just not ready to deal with any drama yet. You know how she is."

He wasn't wrong. Zoe hadn't earned the title Drama Queen by being calm and collected. "Fine." I handed Jack my phone. "Take this and hand it back to me."

"Why?"

"Because then it's not a lie." He handed the phone back, and I texted Zoe that Jack had returned my phone to me.

She texted back, asking me to show the sweater to Jack, which I did. He texted back a thumbs down.

After that, both our phones were silent, and the situation seemed awkward. I sat back down on the love seat. Jack sat on the arm rest.

"Jack, what do you want?"

...

JACK

"What do you mean?" Okay, I knew what she meant, but I'd hoped to avoid any type of relationship conversation. Things were just getting started; why did we have to talk it to death? Plus sometimes, it seemed like my life was the case study for if anything can go wrong it will.

"Don't pull that oblivious guy crap on me. You know what I mean. Are you looking for someone to date every once in a while, or are you looking for a girlfriend? What's the final goal of this relationship experiment we seem to be in?"

I moved off the arm rest to sit beside her. "I don't know. Why can't we just see where it goes?"

"Does that mean you don't want a relationship?"

"No."

She rolled her eyes."Thank you, Mr. Chatty. That cleared everything up."

"I like you. You like me. Neither of us wants to ruin your friendship with Zoe or your open-ended invitation to practically live at my house."

"Which leaves us secretly dating?"

Did I want to say we were dating? I didn't want her dating anyone else, especially not Aiden, and I didn't trust he was out of the picture for good. "Secret dating works for me."

"You know it's two weeks until Christmas, and I don't mean to pressure you, but there will be mistletoe hanging around, and I'd expect the guy I'm dating to kiss me in public if I happen stand under any."

Crap.Trevor had been right. Christmas was a relationship beacon, drawing girls in and making them a needy. "If things between us are good at Christmas, I will honor whatever mistletoe we happen to stand under. Does that work?"

"I guess." She didn't sound happy.

"Allow me to reassure you." I placed my hand on her cheek and turned her face toward mine. She met me halfway, and her lips were soft, and she smelled like flowers, and maybe having a girlfriend who understood me would be nice. If only my brain didn't automatically hunt for all the ways this could go wrong.

...

Monday on the drive to school, I felt nervous, which was stupid. Delia and I had agreed to play it cool at school until we knew what was really going on between us and we were ready to tell Zoe. Which I admit was more me than her.

I met Trevor in the parking lot. "How's Rocky?" I asked.

He held out his cell featuring a picture of Rocky nose deep in a jar of peanut butter. "I will not be eating PB&J's until my mom buys more Jif."

"How'd he get ahold of that?"

"I left it open on the counter this morning after breakfast."

"So it's completely your fault," I pointed out. "You tempted him, and he caved."

"He doesn't have much will power to begin with when it comes to food."

"Buddy likes food, but he prefers socks." I told him about the ever growing sock collection under my bed.

"Your job as a dog owner is to take pictures of your dog doing funny things." I laughed. "I'll work on my camera skills."

As we walked across the quad, I spotted Delia talking to Aiden, and my good mood faded. She caught sight of me, stepped away from Aiden, and waved. He turned to see who she was paying attention to, and he smiled like he knew something I didn't. And I wanted to punch him, which was nothing new. Before, I'd wanted to punch him because he seemed like a rich, entitled asshole. Now he seemed like a rich entitled asshole who was trying to move in on my sort of girlfriend.

The expression on my face must have clued Delia in, because she abandoned her little group and came toward me. "Why do you look angry?"

"Your friend, and I use that term with great irritation, was smirking at me."

"I'm sure he wasn't," Delia said.

"And you defending him isn't helping."

Delia sighed. "Do you want to tell Zoe about us, right now? Because I'll do it if that will prove to you I'm not interested in Aiden."

I wasn't ready to make that move yet. "No. I trust you. I just don't trust him."

Delia headed back to Zoe.

Trevor cleared his throat like he had something to say. "What?"

"I don't get it. You like her. She likes you. Why don't you tell Zoe and let the chips fall where they may? Sure, your sister might be weirded out at first, but after she adjusts, I think she'll be happy for you."

"Something about it doesn't feel right yet." I adjusted the weight of my backpack on my shoulder. "I think Delia is keeping something from me."

"About what?" Trevor asked.

"I don't know. Something about how things ended between her and Aiden doesn't sound right. When was the last time a girl friend-zoned you and you actually wanted to be friends with her afterward?"

"Girls are more in touch with their feelings and all that crap, so maybe Delia just got over it because there wasn't really anything there in the first place."

"Maybe."

Chapter Nineteen

DELIA

I was kind of surprised Jack was so stuck on worrying about Aiden. And I couldn't talk to Zoe about it, and talking to Aiden about it seemed disloyal, so I was stuck mulling it over in my head.

At lunch, Aiden said, "We're still good for my dad's dinner on Friday night, right?"

"Your dad's dinner? I thought you said it would be on a Thursday." Which was a non-date night, so Jack wouldn't even have to know about it.

"Sorry, I had the date wrong. Is that a problem?"

Okay. He was asking me this in the cafeteria in front of Zoe and Grant and anyone else who might be listening. Not good. "Friday might be a problem."

"Why?" Zoe asked. "Do you have a secret boyfriend you're not telling us about?"

I panicked for a moment until I realized she was joking. "I don't know my work schedule yet." Seemed like a reasonable response. "I'll let you know once I have my schedule."

Aiden nodded, but he didn't look pleased. He was my friend, and I wanted to help him, but there was no way Jack would understand if I went someplace with Aiden on a date night. Then again, he wasn't exactly declaring that he wanted to be my one and only. Why were guys so difficult?

Maybe I'd feel him out a bit in art class, see what he thought of me going someplace with a friend on Friday. He didn't have to know who the friend was, and if he wasn't planning on asking me out, did it really matter what I did? I wasn't sure.

When I walked into art class, something about the room was off. It took me a moment to realize half the chairs were missing, or rather, the chairs were back to the normal number. They must have found someone to teach the other art class. A fine layer of disappointment settled around me. I shook it off. Not seeing Jack in class wasn't a big deal. But I had looked forward to it. Was I over investing in this pseudo-relationship? Would Jack even care that we weren't in the same room anymore? Who knew?

"We're back to having some elbow room," the teacher said. "To celebrate, we're going to break out the tabletop easels."

I grabbed an easel from the cart where they were stored and then waited for instructions.

"I've prepared an interesting still life arrangement for you." He hung three Christmas wreathes on magnetic hooks on the white board. Each wreath was covered in miniature ornaments and toys. They'd be fun to draw, but I couldn't imagine wanting to hang them in my house.

After class, I turned in my drawing and headed out into the hall. I kept watch for a certain sandy brown-haired guy, but Jack was nowhere to be seen. I hadn't thought to ask when he worked. I knew I worked tomorrow night, so I guess I'd just wait and see him then. For now, I'd concentrate on me, because focusing on a guy twenty-four hours a day was ridiculous.

This Sunday afternoon was the Christmas Flea Market, where I planned to draw portraits or caricatures of people while Zoe sold cookies and her grandmother sold afghans. When would Zoe want to bake cookies? We'd have to pick a night that fit around my work schedule. Not that she needed my help, but I was usually present for all major baking events.

After our last class, on the walk out to the parking lot, I asked Zoe, "So when does the great bake-off commence for the Christmas Flea Market?"

"I think we should bake Wednesday and Thursday. The cookies will still be fresh, and we won't have do the last minute panic baking."

"Sounds good."

"About Aiden," Zoe said. "This might sound mean, but I don't think you should go to his dad's dinner."

That brought me up short. Like, I literally stopped walking. "Really? Why not?"

She grabbed my elbow and pulled me toward Francine. When she reached the SUV, she looked around like someone might be eavesdropping. "I know you say you're just friends, but to any guy who hears about you going to a party with Aiden on a Friday night, it will sound like you're dating, which means they'll think you're off the market."

I was off the market, sort of... "I agreed to go when it was a Thursday, but I'm not sure I want to go now that it's Friday. Why does that make me feel like a bad person?"

"You're trying to be a good friend, but sometimes you have to do what's right for yourself first," Zoe said. "Jack's friend Trevor is a cute guy who loves his dog, which has to mean he's a good person. Maybe Jack could set you up with him."

I almost laughed out loud. "No. I wouldn't feel comfortable asking Jack to do that."

"That's what best friends are for." Zoe gave me an evil grin, which meant my life was about to become more complicated. She waved at someone coming up behind me. "Hey, Jack. Have you introduced Delia to Trevor?"

Well, this was going to be awkward. I turned around knowing what I'd see. Jack and Trevor walked toward us... both of them looked confused like they didn't know what to say. Then again, neither did I.

"What do you mean?" Jack asked. That seemed to be his go-to line.

Zoe rolled her eyes. "Trevor, this is my best friend, Delia."

"We've met," Trevor said. "Hello, Delia."

"Hello." I glared at Zoe. "Thank you for sponsoring this awkward moment."

"You're welcome," Zoe said. "If you think about it, it makes total sense. You're my best friend. He's Jack's best friend. I think you two should go on a date."

Wow. Now what? Before I could get a word out, Jack said, "Yeah, that doesn't work for me." He reached over, took my hand, and pulled me to stand by his side. "Zoe, there's something you should probably know."

Zoe pointed at our hands. "What are you doing?"

I gave a hopeful smile. "We planned to tell you, but—"

"We didn't want to freak you out," Jack finished for me.

Zoe looked back and forth between us. "Freak out about you two...as in you two together ...you two?"

"You're saying the word two a lot," I pointed out.

"I'm aware of that fact. I just..." She pointed at our hands. "How did this happen?"

Okay...she wasn't taking this as well as I hoped. "With the whole Pie Princess gig and spending time together, things just kind of fell into place."

"But he's my brother," Zoe said, like I might have forgotten that fact.

"Are you shocked or mad?" Trevor asked. "Because it's hard to tell."

"Why do you care?" Zoe snapped.

Trevor held his hands up in surrender. "Just trying to help move this awkward moment along."

"Zoe," I said, "you have every right to go all Drama Queen, but you should know this just happened. It's not like we've been hiding something from you for months or anything."

"How long?" Zoe asked.

"Since the snowstorm Friday night when I stayed and kept her company," Jack said.

"So three days ago," I said. "See. Not long at all."

"Okay." Zoe nodded. "I get that, but if I hadn't tried to fix you up with Trevor, when were you going to tell me?"

Good question. I looked at Jack. He could take the lead on this one.

"I don't know," he said. "When it felt right."

Zoe reached up and rubbed the bridge of her nose. "I can't even...I need some time to think about this." And then she stalked off to Francine.

"Well, shit." Tears filled my eyes. I could not lose my best friend over this. "Now what?"

"It's Zoe," Jack said. "She'll play the drama queen, and then she'll adjust."

"But what do I do? Do I go after her and try to talk her off the ledge? Because that's normally my job."

"Talking to you right now probably wouldn't help," Jack said. "And she has Grant."

I wasn't sure that would work. "Guys aren't usually much help in these situations. Most of the time, they're the ones that cause the situations. And she shouldn't have found out like this."

"She would have acted like this no matter when we told her," Jack said.

"This is fun and all," Trevor said. "But I'm going home." He smacked Jack on the shoulder. "Good luck with Zoe."

"Thanks."

Trevor walked off, and Jack just looked at me. "So...I probably shouldn't go home just yet. Do you want to go grab a coffee?"

I was conflicted. Part of me wanted to run after Zoe, but I knew her. She'd need time to cool off. "Sounds good. We can get a mocha latte to go for her when we're ready to face the music."

...

JACK

Delia and I ended up at a coffee shop where a lot of Wilton students hung out after school. People took notice when we walked in together. After ordering our drinks, we found a table for two in the corner.

"I know you don't mind being the center of attention, but I wish everyone would stop staring." Not that I was ashamed to be seen with her. "It's annoying."

"They're probably speculating on whether we're a couple or not," Delia said.

"Maybe we should help clear that up for them."

"How would we do that?" Delia smiled at me, pretending she didn't understand.

I grabbed the seat of her chair and pulled her over so I could lean in and kiss her. She laughed, but she kissed me back.

"Do you think that worked?" she asked.

"Maybe, but we should try one more just to make sure." I tried to keep a serious expression on my face but couldn't manage it.

"If we must." Delia kissed me again, and the world seemed like a brighter place.

We sat close together, held hands and talked for half an hour. Everything seemed so right.

Delia checked the time on her cell. "Zoe should have cooled down by now."

Armed with a tray of coffee for my entire family and a selection of scones, we headed home. Delia followed me in her truck.

When we pulled up in front of the house, my grandma had Buddy out on his leash. He barked when he saw my truck. I climbed out of the car and set the carry-out tray on the roof before I went over to greet him.

"Hey there, Buddy." I picked him up, and he licked my nose.

Delia came to stand beside me. She'd retrieved the coffee from my car. My grandmother looked at both of us. "Is there something you two want to tell me?"

"I kissed Delia the night of the snowstorm, and now we're dating," I said.

"It's not like we were trying to hide it," Delia added. "It just happened. How mad is Zoe?"

"She's simmered down since she came home. You should be able to talk to her, but I suggest you do it one at a time so she doesn't feel ganged up on."

"Drama Queen," I muttered.

"Is one of those for me?" my grandma asked.

"Of course." Delia held the tray of coffee toward her. "They're all mocha, but the scones are different."

My grandma took a coffee. "Thanks. I'll have a scone later."

We headed toward the house and walked up the front steps.

"I should probably talk to her first," Delia said.

That worked for me. "Just holler when it's my turn or if you need reinforcements."

"Not funny," she said.

Zoe was sitting on the couch crocheting when we walked in. The scarf she worked on looked even more crooked than normal. I veered off into the kitchen and let Delia take the coffee to Zoe.

Before I could even sit down, Zoe hollered, "Jack, get your butt in here."

Okay then. I headed into the living room and tried to gauge the situation. Zoe sipped her mocha latte. That was good. Coffee always made her more rational. I stood by Delia and waited to see what would happen next.

"Do you really like Delia?" Zoe asked.

I nodded. "Yes."

"And you really like Jack?" Zoe said to Delia.

"I do."

She sipped her coffee and frowned. "Then I guess we figure out how to make this work. Because if either of you hurts the other, I won't know whose butt to kick."

"I'm going to run up to my room and let you two do some girly bonding things." I touched Delia's arm. "Come say good-bye before you leave." I leaned over and gave her a quick kiss on the lips.

Delia smiled at me. "Okay."

"I'm resisting the urge to gag," Zoe said.

"It's been no picnic watching you suck face with Grant," I informed her as I scooped up Buddy and headed toward the stairs.

...
DELIA

I sat down next to Zoe. "You're my best friend, and I'd never do anything to upset you. This thing with Jack took me completely by surprise."

"You think you were surprised," Zoe said. "I never in a million years would have put you two together. I blame Betty's."

Couldn't she just be happy for me? "Why don't we talk about something else? Have you figured out which cookies you want to bake for the Flea Market?"

"Let's pull out the cookbooks and see what we can come up with."

I knew Zoe didn't need to look at cookbooks to figure out what kind of cookies she wanted to make, but this gave us something to focus on. Half an hour later, we were talking and laughing like normal...or 90 percent normal. For now, I'd take that.

"I better go home and start dinner," I told Zoe.

"Okay."

Now what? Should I go knock on Jack's door? That would be awkward. I pulled out my phone and texted him telling him to come downstairs.

"So...see you later," I told Zoe as I headed for the front door.

"See you." She sounded almost like herself.

Jack came down the stairs carrying Buddy. "Hey, Zoe, you want to babysit Buddy for a minute?"

"Sure." She smiled and accepted the wiggly brown puppy. "I swear he's gotten bigger."

"I know." Jack came back over to me. "I'll walk you out."

"Okay." We headed out the front door to my truck. Jack had his arm around my shoulders. "So how did it go?" he asked.

"It was a little awkward," I said. "But I think it will be okay." He kissed me good-bye at my truck, and I drove home. When I pulled into the driveway, I was surprised to see my mom's car. She was probably sleeping, but it was nice to have someone else in the house, even if they weren't conscious.

The second surprise came when I found my mom sitting at the kitchen table reading a book. "Hello. I'm surprised you're awake."

"Hello to you, too. I'm too wound up to sleep. I thought reading might help." She closed the book and set it down. "What's new with you?"

"Well, a lot." I sat down and launched into the story of how Jack and I got together and the big reveal in the parking lot with Zoe.

"I knew it," my mom said. "The way he ran off as soon as I came home was a dead giveaway."

I rolled my eyes. "Fine. You were right. Any suggestions on how to handle Zoe?"

"Just continue to be her friend and make time for her."

"I can do that." Just because Jack and I were dating didn't mean my daily life had to change.

Chapter Twenty

DELIA

The moment I walked on to campus the next morning, I realized how wrong I was. I always hung out with Zoe, Grant, and Aiden before school, but Jack intercepted me in the parking lot before I could head over to the quad to meet up in our normal spot.

"Hey there." He grabbed my hand and pulled me close. Trevor was standing there, so I didn't think he planned on kissing me.

"Hey yourself. Good morning, Trevor."

Trevor yawned in response. "Morning."

I was happy to see Jack, and I was thrilled he was so happy to see me, but I felt conflicted. "We better walk over and say hello to Zoe or she'll think I got lost."

Jack frowned. "Will Aiden be there?"

Good question. "I don't know. If he is, I'm sure Grant already told him that you and I are dating, so it shouldn't be a problem."

Jack didn't look like he believed me. "Raise your hand if you think this will be awkward," he said.

All three of us raised our hands, which made me laugh.

"As long as we're all on the same page," Jack said. "Let's go."

We headed over to where Zoe and Grant normally stood. Aiden was suspiciously absent. "Morning," I said to Zoe.

"Morning." She handed me a cup of coffee and then glanced at Jack. "Sorry, you and Trevor will have to provide your own caffeine. I can only carry two cups."

"No problem," Jack said.

We all kind of stood there smiling at each other. "This isn't awkward at all," Trevor said.

Grant snorted.

"Where's your friend?" Jack asked.

"Which one?" Grant replied, even though he had to know Jack was talking about Aiden.

"Adam?" Jack said. "Isn't that his name?" Trevor chuckled.

"Aiden went to ask about a project he's working on," Grant said.

Sure he did. Aiden had said that we'd hang around until one of us started dating someone. I hoped that didn't mean he was going to ditch me as a friend.

"That's a shame," Jack said.

The bell rang, signaling we should head to class, so we shuffled along with the crowd toward the front doors. Jack squeezed my hand. "See you at lunch." And then he took off.

Crap. Since we weren't in art together anymore, the only time I'd see him would be at lunch, but I always ate lunch with Zoe, Grant, and Aiden.

"Would it be weird if Jack sat with us at lunch?" I asked Zoe.

"Yes," she said.

I gave her the side-eye.

"Fine," she said. "We can all sit together like one big dysfunctional family."

Except when lunch rolled around, Jack didn't agree. "We don't have to be one of those couples that eats lunch together every day," Jack said as he sat at the table he shared with Trevor and a few friends. "As long as you're okay with that."

"It's cool. This way I can hang out with Zoe like normal, which should make her happy." I headed back to my table. Sometimes keeping things simple was for the best.

Zoe looked across the room at her brother. "What's wrong?"

"Nothing." I sat down and opened my bottle of water. "Jack is good with keeping lunch the way it's always been, which I'm kind of relieved about. Does that make me a bad girlfriend?"

Zoe shook her head no. "Works for me."

We chatted like normal. Aiden joined us about ten minutes later. "Where have you been?" I asked.

"I'm working on an extra credit project in chemistry," he said. "So what did I miss?"

"I guess Grant told you that Jack and I are dating."

Aiden nodded. "I will keep the negative commentary to myself and ask how it's going."

"So far, so good," I said.

"You never told me if you were going to my dad's award ceremony with me or not," Aiden said.

All three of us stared at him for a moment. How did he not understand that me dating Jack meant I wasn't available to play his fake date?

"As a friend, of course," he added when he noticed the level of scrutiny.

"I don't think Jack would be okay with that." That was the most honest answer I could come up with.

"It's not like you have to ask his permission," Aiden said with a little too much attitude in his tone.

"Let me rephrase that," I said. "I'm not interested in going with you. Jack doesn't even know you asked me. My answer is no."

Aiden pouted for the rest of lunch, making limited conversation.

...

JACK

Maybe I should have eaten lunch with Delia, because watching her sit with Aiden was ticking me off.

"Why does she want to hang out with a guy who friend-zoned her?" I asked Trevor.

"I have no clue. But if she's okay with being his friend, there mustn't have been much going on between them."

Interesting logic. I didn't want to be one of those guys who tried to tell his girlfriend what she could and couldn't do...but seeing her talk with Aiden was like nails on a chalkboard. Maybe if she could explain why she didn't mind hanging out with him, I'd be okay with it.

...

Delia and I tried to figure out when we could spend time together without stepping on Zoe's toes. It wasn't easy. Wednesday after school, she and Zoe baked cookies for the Flea Market. When Zoe left the room to take a call from Grant, I swooped in and pulled Delia into the laundry room.

"What are you doing?" she asked.

"She's taking a break to talk to Grant." I wrapped my arms around her and pulled her close. "So I'm stealing you for a few minutes."

"I like the way you think." She reached up to play with my hair.

I leaned down to kiss her and ignored the rest of the world until the laundry room door smacked me in the back.

"Not cool," I said.

Zoe stood there frowning. "I called your name, but you didn't answer. How was I supposed to know you were in here?"

"Sorry." Delia exited and went back into the kitchen. "Let's get back to work."

"Never mind," Zoe said. "We're almost done anyway."

"You were on a Grant break," Delia reminded her. "So your brother just stopped by to say hello."

"Got it. I pulled the last batch of cookies out of the oven. Feel free to spend more time with Jack." And she stomped off down the hallway.

"The Drama Queen strikes again," I told Delia.

"Should I go after her?"

I didn't want her to. "Do you think you should?"

"She's going to have to adjust to this sooner or later." Her cell buzzed, and she checked it.

"Who's texting you?" I asked.

"Aiden." She shoved the phone in her pocket. "I can text him later."

Before anyone else could interrupt us, I kissed Delia and ignored the voice in my head asking about Aiden. Her phone buzzed two more times. "Do you need to get that?"

"Nope."

"Even if it's Adam?"

"Aiden." She poked me in the chest. "And no."

"What's the deal with him?" I asked.

"What do you mean?"

"I've never been friends with a girl who dumped me," I said. "Help me understand."

"He didn't really dump me. We went on one date. After that, it was all friend stuff."

I wanted to point out she'd been the one who wanted more and he'd said no, which technically meant she'd been dumped.

"We can talk about Aiden, or you can kiss me," she said. "Your choice."

"No contest." I kissed her and did my best to put all thoughts of Aiden out of my head.

...

Thursday at school, I caught Delia in the parking lot before she went over to meet Zoe. "I don't want a repeat of awkward land," I told her.

She laughed. "Uhm...I'm pretty sure that's where we live now."

"It has to get better, right?" I said.

"I hope so." She grabbed my hand. "Come with me."

"No, you go ahead. I'm waiting on Trevor." I gave her a quick kiss. "You working tonight?"

"Yes."

"We could ride together," I suggested.

"Sounds good." She headed off to meet up with Zoe.

Trevor showed up a few minutes later. "Please tell me we're not joining Delia and company."

"Nope."

By the end of the day, I was looking forward to seeing Delia, so I waited by her truck in the parking lot. Seeing her walk out being all chummy with Aiden set me on edge.

She said good-bye to him and smiled at me. "You look annoyed."

"And I'm pretty sure you know why." I glanced in the direction Aiden had gone.

"I don't know how much clearer I can make this. Would it make you feel better to know Aiden asked me to go with him to a dinner on Friday and I said no?"

Why in the hell would that make me feel better? "He asked you out even though he knows we're dating?"

Delia's eyes became huge. "What? No. Not as a date, as a friend, but I said no because I knew you wouldn't like it, and I'd rather spend time with you."

"How do you know he isn't trying to get you back?"

"I can tell you with 100 percent certainty that he isn't interested in dating me."

"How can you know that? What aren't you telling me?"

Delia closed her eyes, and her mouth set in a straight line like she was thinking really hard. "It's hard for me to explain, because I'm keeping something from you about Aiden, because it's not my secret to tell, and it has nothing to do with us dating. If Trevor told you a personal secret, would you share it with someone else?"

"No. But he's my best friend. Aiden is a guy you used to date. There's a difference."

She took a deep breath and blinked her eyes like she was trying not to cry. And now I felt like a dick, but I wasn't wrong. "Delia, just tell me what it is and we can get past this."

"I can't. I haven't even told Zoe."

If she hadn't told Zoe, it must be big.

"I want to tell you, but I'll have to check with Aiden," she said. "I can't tell you unless he says it's okay."

And that's what it all came down to. She cared more about him than she did about me. Big surprise. I should've known this would never work. "Don't bother. And you can drive yourself to work." I turned away from her, ignoring the sniffling sounds that meant she was crying, and jogged over to my car.

I drove home on auto-pilot, not remembering the trip. I only tuned in when I hit the gravel road. This whole idea about dating Delia had been stupid. She was just a girl. Sure, she was cute and funny, but she wasn't anyone special. It's not like I was that into her. I'd find someone else to date after the holidays when the pressure was off. Someone who didn't do strange things to her hair or wear weird sparkly eyeliner. Someone normal.

Buddy doing a happy-furry tap dance when I walked into the house made me feel like my entire world hadn't gone to hell. I picked him up and let him lick my nose. "Come on, boy. Let's get you some food." I filled Buddy's bowl. He made happy crunching chewing sounds as I grabbed a soda from the fridge. Then I changed clothes and headed into work. This should be fun.

Chapter Twenty-One

DELIA

Why was Jack being such a jerk? Though I guess I could see his point. If he hung around with an ex-girlfriend and acted like they were best friends, I wouldn't understand, either.

I smacked the steering wheel as I turned into my driveway. Damn Aiden for putting me in this situation. I should have stuck with my original response when he said I couldn't share with Zoe. But I hadn't. I'd tried to be a good friend, and now being a good friend to Aiden meant screwing up what I had with Jack.

Of course, there were no other cars in my driveway, which meant I was home alone—again. At least I knew there was food in the house. My mom had stocked the kitchen just like I asked. So I could deal with this.

I went inside and hung my backpack up on a hook by the door. Today's emotional crisis called for chocolate. I poured chocolate chips into a coffee mug, added a large glob of peanut butter, and microwaved it on low for fifteen seconds. When I pulled it out and stirred it, the scent of peanut butter and chocolate bliss filled the air. I stirred it and nuked it a few more seconds until it melted together. Then I sat at the kitchen table, put my cell on speaker, and dialed Aiden.

"Hello, Delia. What's up?"

"I am currently scarfing down a mug of melted chocolate chips, and it's your fault."

"Okay. I need more information."

I told him about my fight with Jack.

"So Jack is an idiot."

"No, genius. The root of my problem is I'm keeping your secret. If I could tell Jack the truth, he'd understand."

"You can't," Aiden said. "I'm sorry this is causing you problems, but you can't tell him. He has no reason to keep my secret, and this is a small town, and my dad would kick me out."

"Your mom wouldn't let him do that." It was ridiculous.

"My mom has no power in this relationship. He makes all the decisions."

"Seriously?"

"He gets mad when she buys a different brand of toothpaste. He's not a reasonable man."

Crap. "If I don't tell Jack something, it's over."

"Maybe it's for the best," Aiden said.

And I hated all guys at that moment. "Now you're being a jerk."

"Yeah, but I have a valid reason to act the way I'm acting. Jack is just being an insecure jackass. Do you really want to deal with a guy like that?"

"I gotta go." I ended the call because I didn't want to debate my relationship with Jack, and I needed to get ready for work.

...

JACK

At Betty's, I kept my attention on the people checking out and did my best not to look over at the dessert case. I knew she was there. I heard her laughing and talking with customers. She even sang "Happy Birthday" to some old guy with a walker who didn't seem to know where he was, but he was happy about the pie. It sucked that some people ended up totally out of it. Whatever my grandma's secret was, I hoped she passed it down to me. Maybe I should leave a note for Zoe telling her that if I ended up not knowing who I was, I wanted her to take me sky diving with the provision that she let me pack my own parachute.

At this point, she'd probably push me out of a plane, no questions asked. Why was I thinking these weird thoughts? I checked the clock. Time for my break, but it was too cold to go hang around out back, so I went through the kitchens to the employee lounge, which was really an office Betty never used. I grabbed a soda and a burger on the way. The door slammed behind me before I realized Delia was in the room. I couldn't back out now. Todd sat there, giving me a look like I'd disappointed him. Delia just looked sad.

"What?" I snapped.

"I didn't say a word." Todd stood. "My break's over. See you all later." He balled up his food wrappers, tossed them in the trash, and left.

Shit. I did not know how to handle this. "Should I go eat in my car?" I asked Delia.

"Why would you do that?" she asked. "Oh, wait. I know: because as soon as things get dicey, you run away."

I sat in the seat farthest from her. "Fine. I'll just eat in here. It's not like we can avoid each other."

"Which is why we never should have done this," Delia said.

The bite of hamburger I'd just taken lodged in my throat. I had to take a drink to swallow. "You're probably right."

"No." She sniffed. "I'm just sad and pissed off."

I set my burger down. "Well, I'm not happy, either. You're the one causing the problem."

She slammed her drink down on the table. "Excuse me?"

"You did this. You chose Aiden over me."

"No, I didn't."

How could she not see this?

"I'm not choosing him." Her voice broke, like she was trying not to cry. "I'm just not blabbing someone else's secret that has nothing to do with us."

"As long as you choose to put him first, there is no us." I couldn't make it any clearer than that. "So this is all on you."

The door swung open, and two of the waitresses came in carrying their food. Delia took the opportunity to escape.

...

DELIA

Oddly enough, I was glad I'd run into Jack in the break room, because there was no reason for me to be miserable all by myself. It really ticked me off that he could ignore me all night by keeping his eyes on his customers. I didn't have that luxury since he was right in my line of sight. Still...the fact that he was mad gave me hope. It meant he was still emotionally invested.

I needed to figure out this thing with Aiden. I refused to give up a friend to date a guy, and any guy who asked a girl to do that was a jerk. Jack hadn't asked me to give Aiden up. He just wanted an explanation. An explanation I didn't feel right sharing. It was so freaking frustrating.

Aiden had totally freaked out when I'd brought up telling Jack the truth. Today at school, he'd barely spoken to me. Which was kind of funny. I no longer felt bad about not going to his dad's award dinner.

"Earth to Delia," a male voice said.

I tuned back in to see Todd standing at the dessert counter. "Sorry, I spaced out there for a minute."

"I know something happened between you and Jack and then something else happened which you think screwed it all up, but you're wrong."

"I am?"

"The only time it's really over is when you give up and walk away. Unless one of the two people is an abusive psycho, which I'm pretty sure neither of you are, right?"

"Not the last time I checked."

"So have faith, and it will work out," he said.

"No offense, but what orifice is this logic coming out of?"

Todd laughed. "I met the love of my life in sixth grade. We've already been together more than a decade, and we've had some terrible fights. The key is you have to keep coming back and trying to make it right."

While I wasn't sure about his formula for a successful relationship, he was trying to help. "Thanks for the encouragement. I guess time will tell."

He tapped the countertop like he was playing drums. "That is the sum total of my relationship wisdom. And since I'm by the dessert counter, I might as well get Vicky half of a pecan pie."

"Why half?" I opened the case and pulled out several pieces, setting them in a to-go box.

"If I get a whole pie, she'll complain it's too much. If I take a piece for each of us, it will be gone too quickly. Half a pie ensures she can have a little more than she knows she should but not too much."

"You should start a dating advice youtube channel." And I wasn't joking.

"That's not a bad idea." He accepted the pie and nodded at me. "Have a good night."

"You, too."

Deep inside me, a small voice kept whispering if Jack thought I was special, he should be willing to fight for me. To try and make it work. Apparently, that wasn't the case, because he wasn't trying very hard to make this right.

...

JACK

After work, I sat at the kitchen table eating cookies, which were probably meant for the flea market, but that was too bad.

My mom and grandmother joined me.

"That is not a happy face," my mom said. "What's wrong?"

"Delia and I had a fight."

"I hope it wasn't something big," my grandmother said. "The holidays are coming, and I expect everyone to be cheerful and bright."

I laughed. "I make no guarantees."

"I'm not dreading Christmas this year, like I have the last two years," my mom said in a quiet voice, like she was confessing something.

"Thanksgiving was kind of fun this year," I said.

"I think it's time for us to enjoy our lives again," my mom said. "I think they'd want that for us."

My eyes burned, but I nodded in agreement, not trusting my voice.

"I know they'd want us to be happy," said my grandmother.

My grandma and mom headed into the living room, and I camped out at the kitchen table doing my homework. Zoe came in to grab a snack.

"In case you care, Delia called me, and she isn't happy."

I erased a mistake on my paper. "Not my fault."

"How is it not your fault? You're the one being a jerk."

"No. She's the one keeping a secret."

"What does that matter if it doesn't have anything to do with you?"

"Okay, Miss High and Mighty, if Grant spent time with his ex, insisted they were just friends and kept a secret for her, would you be okay with that?"

Zoe frowned. "Oh...when you put it that way."

"Do you understand now?"

"Yes, but this is Delia we're talking about. She'd never do anything to hurt anyone on purpose. Maybe that's why she can't tell you, because it would cause problems for Aiden."

"If she doesn't choose me over him, why should I bother with her?"

Zoe muttered something under her breath as she left the room.

This was exactly why I never should have kissed her in the first place. It was probably better that it fell apart now rather than six months from now. There wasn't that much to get over. In a few weeks, kissing her would be a distant memory.

My cell buzzed. It was a text from Trevor with a sad face. Rocky was wearing a cone of shame, and his nose was swollen to twice its normal size.

I called Trevor. When he answered, I said, "Poor guy, what happened?"

"Spider bite. He's on steroids. The vet said it should be better within twenty-four hours."

"What's with the cone of shame?" I asked.

"He isn't supposed to scratch. I'm holding an icepack on his nose right now."

"So Rocky had a crap day, too." I'd meant it as a joke, but it fell flat.

"You know Delia is a pretty cool girl. Most people blab crap all over the internet. She's keeping a secret for a guy who was kind of a jerk to her, just because it's the right thing to do."

"I hate Aiden." And I wasn't lying. "His stupid secret has screwed this whole thing up."

Trevor was silent.

"What?"

"Nothing. I've said my piece. You can do what you want. Rocky's falling asleep standing up, so I'm going to take him into the living room and help him up onto the couch before he passes out."

I loved that dog. "Will someone be home with him tomorrow?"

"Yeah, my mom's going to take a sick day. She says she took days to take care of me, and Rocky is her baby, too."

"Cool. See you tomorrow."

I picked up Buddy, who'd fallen asleep by my feet. He yawned. I thought about Delia and what Zoe had said. Had I made a mistake? It wasn't my fault she'd agreed to keep an ex's secret. But I'm also pretty sure there wasn't a guy on the planet who'd be okay with a girl being that tight with a guy who'd friend-zoned her.

...

DELIA

I woke up the next morning to the suckiest Friday ever. Too wound up to sleep last night, I'd started a new craft project, which in hindsight was incredibly stupid because then I didn't go to bed until one. There wasn't enough coffee in the world to wake me up this morning.

And I didn't want to go to school. I didn't want to see Jack, or Aiden, or pretty much anyone. I wanted to hide under my blankets all day. Unfortunately, that wasn't an option.

I texted Zoe that I'd be a little late and she shouldn't wait for me on the quad. That way, I could avoid seeing Aiden, because rational or not, I was angry at him. And I didn't want to bump into Jack, either.

Fate mocked me as Jack pulled into a parking spot right next to mine when I was getting out of my car. He didn't acknowledge me. He just stalked off. At least I didn't have work with him tonight.

I went through the motions during class. I was grateful when lunch arrived and Aiden didn't show up at our table. One less problem to deal with.

"Where's the fourth member of the band?" Zoe asked Grant.

"A new guy started today. His dad works for the same law firm as Aiden's dad, so Aiden was volunteered as his guide to all things Wilton."

"Maybe he'll be cute and single," Zoe said.

"I'm sitting right here," Grant said.

"Not for me," Zoe said. "For Delia."

"Nope. I have enough guy issues. I just want to make it through Christmas without drama. People get all clingy over the holidays because they don't want to be alone, and I don't need that."

Aiden entered the cafeteria, and the volume increased. The new guy was hot. He was a few inches taller than Aiden and on the slim side. His dark complexion, sharp cheekbones, and close-cropped hair made him look like a model. And he made the Wilton uniform look fashionable, which was quite the achievement.

"I changed my mind," I said to Zoe. "I want one."

"You and every other female in this room," Grant said.

Oblivious to the attention they were drawing, Aiden came over and smiled as he sat down. "Time for more names, even though I don't expect you to remember everyone. This is my best friend Grant, his girlfriend Zoe, and our friend Delia. And this," Aiden pointed at the new guy, "is Devon."

Devon nodded at all of us as he sat down. "Nice to meet you." He glanced around. "How long will it take for everyone to stop staring at me?"

"Give everyone a week, and they'll move on to something else," I said.

"Why a week?" Aiden asked.

"Seems logical. And just so you know, you're on my shit list." I probably shouldn't have said that in front of the new guy, but my filter was off due to lack of sleep.

Aiden blushed. "Sorry I was a jerk yesterday."

Devon looked back and forth between Aiden and me.

He seemed surprised. "You dated?"

"How did you know that?" I asked.

"There is a certain level of awkwardness," Devon said. "That only occurs between people who have dated."

"I guess we sort of dated," I said. "But not really."

"Interesting." Devon leaned toward Aiden. "We should go to that awards banquet together tonight, and I can tell you about the girl I dated before I figured things out."

Aiden froze, and then he shrugged. "Okay."

Had Devon just asked Aiden on a date? I wasn't sure. Grant and Zoe didn't seem to think anything was going on, but then again, they didn't know what I knew. I wanted to drag Aiden off somewhere and ask him what was going on, but I couldn't do that without arousing suspicion.

And then I remembered something. "I wanted to ask everyone's opinion on something." Reaching into my backpack, I pulled out the project I'd started last night when I couldn't sleep. "I'm trying to come up with a new product to sell at the Christmas Flea Market, and I need to know if this is a dumb idea." I laid out the dog collars I'd made from weaving strips of fabric together. "Can you tell what they are?"

"They're too big to be bracelets," Aiden said.

"Not if you wrapped them around twice," said Zoe.

I picked one up and wrapped it around my wrist twice. "Not a bad idea, but they're supposed to be dog collars."

"That makes much more sense," Aiden said.

"So they work?" I asked. "Because I'm not feeling up to doing portraits."

"Yes," Zoe said. "They're pretty cool."

"Good." I picked up the small red, black, and gold collar I'd made for Buddy. "I'll be right back."

I stood and walked over to where Jack sat with Trevor and held the collar out to Jack. "I'm selling dog collars at the Christmas Flea Market, and I made one for Buddy."

Jack took the collar and studied it for a moment. "Iron Man's colors?"

I nodded.

"Thanks," he said.

And the conversation was dead in the water, so I turned around and walked back to Zoe. I should have given the collar to her. What had I been thinking?

The bell rang, and it was time to go to our next class. I kept a lookout for Jack but didn't see him for the rest of the day. I did notice Aiden talking with Devon and some other guys on campus that he hadn't hung around before. Some of those guys were holding hands. Maybe Aiden was ready to be who he really was. If he did that, then I wouldn't have to keep his secret anymore.

Chapter Twenty-Two

JACK

The new guy seemed to draw a lot of attention. At the end of the day, he stood with a group of guys in the parking lot. Trevor and I nodded at him when he looked over at us, and he nodded back. Good to know he wasn't stuck up.

When we were halfway to our cars, Trevor said, "This may sound weird, but I'm glad that guy is gay."

I stopped walking. "What?"

"Dude, he's too good looking. I don't want to compete with that."

"I get it, but how do you know he's gay?"

"He's hanging out with Josh and Eric, who've been together forever. He hasn't checked out any of the girls who've stopped to talk to him."

"Huh." I continued walking, and when I reached my car, I stood so I could observe Devon and the guys he spoke to. "Aiden was showing him around today, so Zoe probably has the inside scoop."

"Aiden is over there talking to him," Trevor said.

And that's when it clicked into place. "Wait a minute. That must be the secret Delia didn't want to share and the reason she's fine being friends with Aiden. He's gay."

"That would make sense," Trevor said.

I looked around the parking lot for Delia's truck but couldn't spot it. "I need to talk to her." Pulling out my cell, I called her and waited. She didn't pick up.

"She's probably driving," Trevor said.

If the secret was that Aiden was gay but not out yet, then everything made sense. Where was Zoe? I spotted my sister standing by Francine.

I jogged over to her. "Where's Delia?"

"I think she went to buy more fabric for dog collars. Why?"

I told her about my Aiden theory.

She blinked. "Oh my gosh. That would make so much sense."

"Now that I understand why Delia kept his secret, how do I make this right?"

"Do you work tonight?" Zoe asked.

"No. I don't think she does, either."

"Go. Talk to her. Work this out, and then I'm punching both of you for putting me through this drama."

I'd put Delia in a hard spot when she was trying to do the right thing by Aiden. Now, I wanted to do something nice for her. But what? And then it hit me. "I need you to keep Delia busy for a few hours. Can you do that?"

"Why?" Zoe asked.

I told her my plan and then ran back to Trevor because I was going to need his help to make this work. Maybe not everything in my life had to go bad. Maybe it was time for me to stop running away...time to work at something and make sure it went right.

...

DELIA

I stood in line at Goodwill with some clothes made of interesting fabrics that would make cool dog collars while the lady in front of me argued about the price of an item. My mind drifted to Aiden. Devon was into him, and I couldn't imagine anyone who was alive and breathing not being into Devon. He was hot and funny and very at ease with himself. He'd do Aiden a world of good.

If Aiden and Devon got together, then I wouldn't have to be his secret keeper anymore. I could tell Jack the truth and then maybe things would work out in my favor. My cell buzzed as I paid for my purchases. I checked the text. It was from Zoe. She wanted me to meet her at the Art of Tea. It's not like I had any other plans.

Zoe already had a table when I arrived. And she'd started a painting, which was beyond terrible. She'd mixed lime green slashes with bubblegum pink circles and orange triangles. Zoe didn't paint. And this painting proved why she never should. She turned to me with a giant grin on her face. "What do you think?" She gestured at the atrocity. "I finally did what you told me to do. I just went with my gut."

The color combination burned my eyes, but she was so excited. "I can't believe you're painting."

"I wanted to come up with a really cool Christmas gift for Grant. What do you think? Is it too feminine?"

And here was my way in. "Since it's for Grant, I think you should choose a darker color pallet."

"Maybe you're right." Zoe turned back around and studied the painting. "Should I add a really dark purple?"

"Go over the pink with the dark purple," I suggested. "I'm going to go grab a raspberry tea. Do you need a refill?"

"No. I'm good."

I headed up to the line and ordered a large tea. It looked like we might be here a while.

Two hours later, Zoe's painting wasn't horrible. I'd steered her toward purples, blues, and black. Her shapes were a bit off balance, but it wasn't the eyesore it had been when she started. Lesson learned. I would never encourage her to paint again. She'd been right to stick with baking and crocheting.

On the drive home, I thought about the upcoming flea market. How many collars should I make for Sunday? I probably wouldn't need more than a dozen, and I'd be lucky if I sold half of those. At least they were fun and cheap to make. Maybe that was the key to being a happy artist—low cost, enjoyable-to-make art that had commercial appeal. Everything didn't have to be flashy and showy. To commemorate this new discovery, maybe it was time for me to pick a new hair color. I could scale the pink back to strawberry blond. Not that my pink hair was a cry for attention... Okay, maybe it had been...but maybe I needed to be happy with myself for a little while. Not that I'd give up my sparkly lip gloss and eyeliner, because those were awesome, but it wouldn't hurt if I blended a tiny bit better with the population. Then a guy might notice me for who I was rather than the bright pink color of my hair.

When I pulled into my driveway, I was happy to see my mom's car. Maybe I wouldn't be eating alone tonight. When I let myself in the house, I smelled barbecue. Yum.

"Hello?" I walked into the kitchen and opened the Crock-Pot, which was full of barbecued beef. Where was my mom? I listened but didn't hear the giant fan noise from upstairs that meant she was sleeping.

"Mom?" I headed into the living room and heard a door slam in the back of the house.

"Delia, did you see what's in the Crock-Pot?" My mom came toward me, smiling. "I just need to put some rolls in the oven."

A hammering sound came from the back of the house. "What was that?"

"What was what?" My mom put her arm around my shoulders and propelled me toward the kitchen.

"Is Dad working on something out back?"

"What? No." She pointed at the fridge. "Grab the rolls and set the temperature on the oven."

Something was going on. I opened the refrigerator and smiled at the six cardboard tubes stacked on the shelf. Who knew having food around the house would make me feel so happy? I picked out the kind of rolls that pulled apart in layers and set the oven to the right temperature.

My cell buzzed. It was a text from Jack. Crap. What was I going to do about him? "I'm here. Can we talk?" And then I heard a knock on the front door.

That didn't give me a lot of options, since he knew I was home. So I walked into the foyer and checked out the window. Sure enough, Jack stood on my porch. I opened the door and waved him in. "We were just about to eat, if you want to join us."

"That sounds great, but can we talk first?"

"Sure." I led him into the living room and sat on the couch.

He pointed toward the back door that led to my studio. "Let's talk out there."

"Why?"

He grabbed my hands and tugged me to my feet. "Humor me."

Why was he acting so weird? Did he think I was going to freak out and he didn't want my mom to hear?

"You're up to something," I said as he led me toward the door.

"I am." He smiled. "I wanted to do something for you to show you how special you are and that I think this relationship is worth fighting for."

Holy crap. What had he done?

He stepped in front of me and opened the door to my studio. Except it didn't look like my studio anymore. I stepped through the door and tried to take it all in. A large shaggy area rug covered most of the concrete floor. A well worn brown leather couch sat against one wall. There was a wooden coffee table in front of it. Clear Christmas lights were draped from the ceiling beams, and the far wall was covered with bright pink curtain panels—the same color as my hair. A coffeemaker sat on what looked like an antique end table.

"Delia?" Jack said, like he wasn't so sure of himself anymore.

And I burst into tears.

"Oh, crap. My grandma has other furniture we can use. Or I can take it all down."

"What? No. I love it." I threw my arms around him in a hug.

He hugged me back and kissed the top of my head. "Then why are you crying?"

How to explain without sounding like I was whining? "Everything I do has always just been me. It took me weeks to clean this garage out so I could have a place to paint. I always wanted to make it nice, but it just seemed like so much work. Thank you."

"You're welcome." He leaned down and kissed me. It was a slow, sweet kiss that ended too soon. "This is my way of apologizing for being a jerk about you being friends with Aiden and keeping his secret, which I'm pretty sure I figured out."

"If you were hanging out with an ex and acting like it was no big deal, I'd probably be annoyed, too."

"So we're good now?" he asked.

There was only one other possible complication. "What about Zoe?"

"She plans on punching both of us for putting her through the drama, but other than that, she's okay."

"Good." And then it clicked. "Please tell me her terrible painting was just your way of keeping me busy so you could do all this."

"It was," he said.

"Thank God. New rule from now on: Zoe isn't allowed to paint." It seemed like the last barrier between us had fallen. "So does this mean I'm welcome at all your family gatherings but I'm no longer a family member?"

"Pretty much, because that would be kind of incestuous and creepy."

"Agreed."

"There's one more thing." He pointed at a box on the coffee table. It took me a minute to realize it was a box of hair highlighter.

I laughed. "You're really going to let me highlight your hair?"

"I would," he said, "because I trust you."

"Thank you, but I'm pretty sure you're perfect just the way you are."

A knock sounded on the door. "Hello? Can I come in without interrupting anything embarrassing?" my mom called out.

"Yes."

She walked in and said, "Now, when he does something stupid, which all guys do sooner or later, and you want to smack him in the head with a frying pan, just remember he showed up and did all of this for you as a surprise. So he's probably a keeper."

"Mom."

"Please, I'm your mother. It's my job to pass along feminine wisdom. Now I'm about to take the rolls out of the oven, so come eat."

I sighed, knowing my mom was going to say something to embarrass the crap out of me, but that was okay. I needed one more reassurance from Jack.

"No matter what happens, even if we fight, promise me you won't run away."

"No. I'm done running. You're stuck with me. And if I do freak out and need some time to myself, I will always come back."

"Like a boomerang?" I asked.

"Weird comparison, but yeah."

I would so have to tell Aiden about that later. "Okay, Boomerang Boyfriend. Here's your first test. You do realize we'll have to double date with Grant and Zoe."

"The compulsion to run is strong." He pulled me toward the kitchen. "Let's eat, and then we'll negotiate who we double date with."

"It's non-negotiable," I said. "Best friends double date."

"Then we need to find Trevor a girlfriend as soon as possible."

Acknowledgments

I'd like to thank my family for all their encouragement and support.

About the Author

Chris Cannon lives in Southern Illinois with her husband and several furry beasts. She believes coffee is the Elixir of Life. Most evenings after work, you can find her sipping caffeine and writing fire-breathing paranormal adventures, romantic comedies or paranormal cozy mysteries. You can find her online at www.chriscannonauthor.com.

Also by Chris Cannon

Going Down In Flames
Bridges Burned
Trial By Fire
Fanning The Flames
Burning Bright

Mysteries of Mystic Hills
Murder in Mystic Hills
Double Trouble in Mystic Hills
SpellBound in Mystic Hills

Sweet Snarky Romance Series
The Boyfriend Bet
Boomerang Boyfriend
The Dating Debate
99% Faking It

Watch for more at https://www.chriscannonauthor.com/.

www.ingramcontent.com/pod-product-compliance
Lightning Source LLC
Chambersburg PA
CBHW052134170626
46812CB00004B/1400